R.L. STINE'S
MONSTERVILLE

CABINET
OF SOULS

INTRODUCED BY R.L. STINE

ADAPTED BY JO ANN FERGUSON
FROM A SCREENPLAY WRITTEN BY
BILLY BROWN & DAN ANGEL

SCHOLASTIC INC.

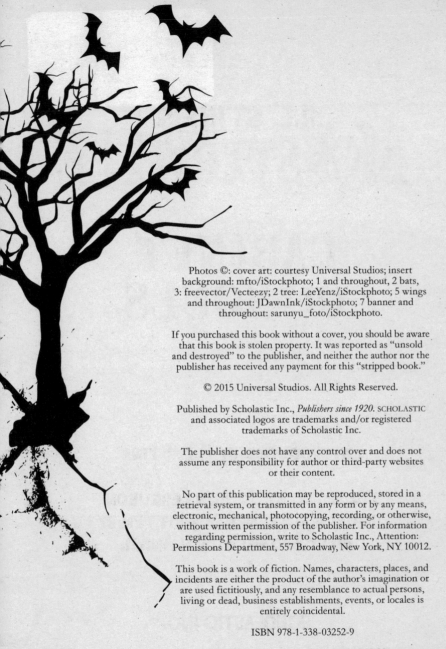

ISBN 978-1-338-03252-9

12 11 10 9 8 7 6 5 4 3 2 1   16 17 18 19 20

Printed in the U.S.A.   40
First printing 2016

INTRODUCTION

BY R.L. STINE

MONSTERS ARE REAL.

You may think they exist only in imagination and in your darkest dreams. But then how do you explain the howls in the woods behind your house late at night? Or the bloodred eyes peering through your bedroom window just as you're about to fall asleep?

Can you explain the strange paw prints in your garden? The shifting shadows behind you as you walk to school? The low growls you hear when you open the door to the basement?

Yes, monsters are real. And if you pretend they don't exist, you may pay a terrifying price.

Take Beth, for example.

She and her friend Kellen and their high school friends are excited when the traveling Hall of Horrors sets up in their little town of Danville. They can't wait to be scared by the ghouls and zombies and ugly creatures that inhabit the hall. The owner, Dr. Hysteria, is quite a showman.

Or maybe he isn't. Maybe the show isn't all in fun. Maybe Beth shouldn't explore the back halls of Dr. Hysteria's theater. Maybe she shouldn't open the strange cabinet she finds in a hidden room.

Beth and her friends should believe in monsters. They shouldn't think that scares are always in fun.

Beth is about to find out that she doesn't live in Danville. Beth lives in . . . *Monsterville.*

HALLOWEEN ... LAST YEAR

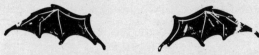

"TRICK OR TREAT! TRICK OR TREAT!"

Little kids' voices called from front porches along the streets of Federson Township. Ghosts and superheroes ran from house to house alongside bunnies and monsters.

Nobody noticed the real monster walking down the street.

The girl was about fifteen, with curly blonde hair. She wore a maroon hoodie with FEDERSON HIGH SCHOOL printed across the front. She was alone.

She stopped by a jack-o'-lantern near the sidewalk. It wore a grin.

She frowned.

Raising her foot, she smashed the pumpkin. Once, twice, and again until it was nothing but orange pulp.

The girl pulled her hood up over her head. When she looked up, wondering if anyone had seen her obliterate

1

the smiling pumpkin, her eyes had changed. They were as green as a cat's, and slitted.

She wasn't a cat.

And she wasn't a girl anymore, either.

She raced between two houses and into the woods behind them. She stumbled, fell, and then kept running. Sometimes on two feet, sometimes on four. Her body wasn't her own anymore. It belonged to someone else.

To *something* else.

When the change was complete, her cry of horror echoed through the night.

She wasn't a cat.

She wasn't a girl.

She was a monster with pointed ears and a gremlin's face.

With a cry, she vanished into the night, trying to escape what she had become. But she feared there was no escape.

Not ever.

CHAPTER 1

ONE YEAR LATER ...

Kellen Huston strolled along Danville's main street. There were little white lights strung between the red and orange and yellow leaves in the trees.

It was Danville's harvest festival, and everyone in town had gone all out. Little kids were dressed in costumes of all sorts. A bumblebee and a cowgirl and a spaceman ran from shop to shop, looking up at the gruesome masks hung on racks waiting for older kids who might dare to put them on.

The street had been transformed into a parade of booths. Food and crafts were for sale everywhere Kellen looked. The gazebo in the town square was decorated with pumpkins waiting to be lit as soon as the sun set. Mayor Smith had been the one and only judge for the pumpkin-carving contest. Unsurprisingly, the winning pumpkin looked more caring than scaring. Mayor Smith wasn't what you'd call a risk taker.

Kellen could understand that. He'd never been one to take a risk, either. He was the safe guy. The guy next door. The one who wasn't ugly, but wasn't really handsome, either.

Not like Beth Hooper. She was beautiful. Her hair was blonde. Her eyes twinkled whenever he made her laugh.

He was just Kellen. Good-old, safe Kellen . . . who was too scared to tell her how he really felt about her.

Tonight, that was all going to change . . . he hoped.

"Hey, Kellen!"

He looked over his shoulder. It was Luke Brody, his best friend. Luke had a goofy sense of humor. Most of the time Kellen thought he was pretty funny, but not tonight. Tonight he wanted to see Beth. Where was she? She'd said she'd be here.

"I got gummy bears and churros," called Luke as he hurried to catch up with Kellen. He'd stuck four or five gummy bears into the churro he held.

Luke was always hungry and always up for adventure—at least when it came to food. "Combo bite."

Kellen grimaced. "That's gross."

"What's so gross about it?" Luke asked, around a mouthful of churro. A gummy bear dribbled from his lower lip as he spoke.

Kellen grinned. That was Luke for you.

Kellen's phone chirped. He pulled it out of his jacket and looked at the screen.

Where are you guys?

A text from Beth. Okay!

"Who are you texting?" Luke asked, elbowing Kellen as he craned his neck to look at the screen.

"Dude . . . ," Kellen said, tilting his phone away.

"What?"

"Geez . . ." He walked away, texting his answer back to Beth. He wasn't going to lose his nerve this time.

Not again.

Beth leaned against the sink in the ladies' room and waited for a reply to her text. She didn't have anything else to do while she waited for Nicole to finish putting on her makeup. Not that Nicole needed much. She was pretty, with long, black hair and a wide smile.

Nicole worried about how she looked all the time. Sure, Beth liked to look good, but she wasn't obsessed like Nicole. She liked to dress comfortably and casually, and she didn't mess much with her blonde hair.

Her phone buzzed. It was Kellen.

At the candy apple stand.

"Hurry up, Nicole. They're waiting for us." She typed a quick answer.

Be there in two minutes.

Nicole gave her one of those looks. The kind that said Nicole knew so much more than Beth did about the world—especially when it came to how boys think. "C'mon, Beth. You know it's always better to make boys wait."

Beth rolled her eyes at Nicole. But it wasn't worth arguing over, so she sent another text.

Make that five minutes.

Beth was psyched for the festival. She hoped something exciting would happen soon. Something more exciting than watching Nicole put on mascara . . . again. After all, it was only a few days until Halloween. Beth wanted something creepy. A good old-fashioned scarefest.

Beth sighed. What were the chances of that happening in Danville?

CHAPTER 2

KELLEN AND LUKE stood IN FRONT of the harvest festival's dunk tank. Luke held three balls. He bounced one in his right hand, preparing to let it fly.

Kellen edged back a step and looked around for Beth. Then he reminded himself that he'd better keep his eye on the ball . . . and Luke. Even when Luke aimed, the ball could land pretty much anywhere.

Kellen had two candy apples held carefully in his hands. The first apple was decorated with orange candy and looked like a pumpkin. The other was a classic—complete with sugary, sticky red covering. He hoped Beth would say yes to one . . . and to a date with him.

No chickening out tonight.

He heard a cackle. A green-faced witch—Ms. Sarkosian, their history teacher—was perched on a stool above the tank. If anyone hit the target bull's-eye to her left, that seat would collapse, dropping her into the water.

"C'mon, spaghetti arm," Ms. Sarkosian taunted. "Throw it."

Luke threw the ball. It went high, hitting the tarp behind the target.

"I curse your lousy aim," Ms. Sarkosian called in her witchiest voice.

Kellen ignored her. He had more important matters on his mind.

"Hey, listen . . ." He looked Luke in the eye. "When Beth gets here, maybe you can sort of not hang around for a little bit."

"What do you mean, 'not hang around'?" Luke asked.

The witch called, "Throw the ball, bozo."

Luke threw again. And missed again.

As Ms. Sarkosian cackled, Kellen gave Luke a *get a clue* look. "Dude . . ."

"Are you kidding me?" Luke's smile disappeared. For once, he was as serious as a stomachache.

"What?"

"You've been planning on making your move ever since Beth moved in next door. That was, like, ten years ago, right? But you chicken out every time."

Kellen frowned. "Maybe this time I won't chicken out."

Luke gave him a look that said *yeah, right*. Then he looked back at the witch as she shouted, "Throw it before it hatches!"

This time, Luke hit the target squarely. The stool dropped Ms. Sarkosian straight into the tank. She came up sputtering, her hat floating next to her. Her green face makeup dripped down her cheeks.

She jammed her hat back on her head. "Bet you can't do that again!" She shook a finger at him as she spit out a mouthful of water.

"Sorry, Ms. Sarkosian," Luke called.

That was the moment Beth and Nicole emerged from the crowd. "Hey, guys," Beth said, with the smile that made Kellen's day.

Luke grinned at Nicole, who looked gorgeous . . . as always. "Wassup?"

But Nicole only had eyes for Kellen. "Hi, Kellen."

"Hi . . ." He looked at Beth and held out the orange candy apple. "I thought you might like this."

Beth took it with a laugh. "Oh, that's so incredibly sweet of you. Thank you."

Nicole's smile faded. "Is that one for me?" she asked.

Kellen glanced at the other candy apple in his hand, the one he'd planned to eat while he and Beth talked. He didn't want to hurt Nicole's feelings.

"Well . . . sure." He held it out to her.

Nicole didn't take it. "I don't eat sweets."

Now it was Kellen's turn to be embarrassed. "Okay . . ."

"I'll take it," Luke said, never one to let free food go to waste.

"Fine. Here." Kellen handed the candy apple to Luke as Nicole wandered off to look at some of the Halloween costumes for sale.

Luke started to take a big bite. He stopped when Kellen motioned for him to *go away.*

Luke finally got it. "I shall go and find the candy-apple eating area."

That left Kellen right where he wanted to be: with Beth. Just the two of them.

All he had to do now was open his mouth and ask her to go out with him. Easy, right?

He'd never been so nervous in his life.

Beth wasn't paying attention. She was laughing at Luke. He was such a goofy guy. She nibbled at the orange candy apple and looked back at Kellen. He was acting weird tonight. She was used to weird with Luke, but Kellen was usually a guy she could depend on.

"I was . . . I was thinking, for Halloween," Kellen said, "we could get a bunch of scary movies and do a marathon."

"That could be fun," she replied. "I'll start an event page. We could make it a party."

Kellen hesitated, his face going blank for a moment. That wasn't exactly what he'd had in mind.

Then his smile returned. "Yeah . . . yeah . . ."

Beth laughed.

"What?" he asked.

"This just reminded me. Do you remember when we were trick-or-treating—I think we were, like, seven—anyway, you were sitting on the curb and you were crying because this big kid stole your little pumpkin full of Halloween candy."

Kellen shook his head. "No, no, no. I was—"

"You were crying!" She laughed.

"I don't think I was *crying*."

Luke heard Kellen's voice raised in protest. He glanced back at him and Beth, and then ambled over to Nicole, who'd found a seat on a bench nearby. All by herself. She looked miserable.

Luke sat beside her. "Sure you don't want some?" he asked, holding out the candy apple.

"No." She said it with a half smile, but her eyes were sad.

He had to do something. Something to make her laugh again. It was what he was good at.

"It doesn't bite," he said, offering her the apple again.

She didn't take it. She was too busy looking at Beth and Kellen.

"Look," Beth ordered Kellen, showing him a picture on her phone. The screen showed a much younger Kellen sobbing and wiping tears off his cheek.

"Great," he said. "You've got a picture of me crying on your phone."

She giggled. "Yeah. My mom just scanned a bunch of old photos. Tons."

"I'm glad my humiliation has been preserved for the digital age."

She smiled and patted his arms. "Blackmail for days."

"Oh, gosh. I know. I know."

She looped her arm through his. Together, they started toward the town square.

Just then, a terrified shout tore through the night. *"Get it off! Get it off me!"*

CHAPTER 3

"LUKE!" KELLEN SAID, "HE'S OVER there. What has he done to himself now?"

Beth and Kellen pushed through a crowd in front of a hot dog stand.

The shouts didn't stop. "Get it off!"

As they rounded the street corner, they saw what Luke was shouting about. Somehow he had stuck the candy apple to his hair and the side of his face. He was acting as if a black widow spider had crawled up his cheek.

Nicole looked like she wanted to disappear. "Help me!" she mouthed.

Beth shook her head and sighed. "I'd better go save Nicole."

"Yeah," Kellen agreed. "I'll rescue Luke."

They were interrupted by a voice coming from a loudspeaker in the middle of the square.

"Attention, everyone! Right this way, please."

That was all the invitation Nicole needed. She stood up, grabbed Beth's arm, and started to follow the crowd toward the gazebo in the center of the square.

"Right this way," the deep voice repeated.

As the four teenagers drew closer, they spotted Mayor Smith standing in the gazebo. As always, he was holding a handful of index cards. He never spoke in public without his cards.

The sheriff and a redheaded woman stood next to him. As the crowd approached, Mayor Smith tapped the microphone. Feedback squealed, and everyone covered their ears.

"Good evening, guys and ghouls." The mayor paused to chuckle at his own lame joke. No one else laughed, so he explained, "'Cause it sounds like *girls*. Okay, moving on," he continued, turning to his next index card. "I want to officially welcome everyone to our annual Harvest—" He flipped from one card to the next. "—and Halloween Festival here in Old Town."

Everyone applauded.

"Now," Mayor Smith said, "I'm going to hand the mic over to—" He flipped to another card. "—Nora Fishbean . . ."

The redhead grabbed the mic. "Nora *Fishbine*."

"Fishbine," the mayor said. "Of Nora's Dance and Ballet Academy." He switched to a cheesy vampire voice.

"Who will be the spooky mistress of the very spooky Halloween dance contest!" He grinned. "Dracula, get it?"

"Thank you, Mr. Mayor," Nora Fishbine said.

"Count Dracula," added the mayor.

Nora shot him an annoyed look. "Yes, that was clear." Her smile returned. "May I invite all the contestants to make their way to the dance floor?" Nora stepped back, and the mayor gestured to the right.

A tent had been set up over a wooden floor. Paper pumpkins hung from the top, and jack-o'-lanterns sat on top of hay bales at each corner. A DJ stood by with his equipment, and a table waited for the judges—the mayor and Sheriff Wilson.

Beth looked at Kellen. "Should we?"

Kellen squirmed a little. Dancing wasn't his strong suit. In fact, he preferred to stand back and leave the dancing to others.

"Um . . ." he said.

"Oh, c'mon!" Beth bounced up and down. "Don't be so shy!"

As they walked off, Luke grinned at Nicole. "It's about time everyone got to see my dance moves." He grabbed her arm. "C'mon. C'mon."

About a dozen couples—all of them around fifteen or sixteen—stepped onto the floor. Everyone else gathered around to watch.

Ms. Fishbine stepped to another microphone as the sheriff and mayor took their seats. "All right, everyone," she said. "In keeping with the Halloween spirit, I'll call out different themes, and the dancers will make up their own dances. There's no right or wrong. Just be creative."

In the front row, Beth smiled at Kellen. "Sounds like fun," she said.

His face said he didn't think so, but she patted his arm and pulled him out to the dance floor.

"Everybody ready?" The DJ played a quick riff, and the crowd cheered.

"Let's dance," Kellen said.

The music started with a good beat. Beth put up her hands and began rocking to it. Everyone else started to dance to the beat, but Kellen didn't move. The other dancers seemed to be having fun. Kellen began to bob his head.

Beth poked his arm. Her expression told him that she wasn't going to dance by herself. Kellen started to move. He wasn't a bad dancer. In fact, he was pretty good at keeping up with Beth. He grabbed her waist and lifted her up as they turned around.

"Not bad," she said, slapping him playfully on the chest.

"I don't like showing off my moves to everyone," he said, smiling at her.

Nora Fishbine held out her arms, hands down, and called, "Dance like a zombie!"

Beth and Kellen raised their arms and walked toward each other as if they'd just gotten a craving for brains. Around them, everyone was laughing and acting like the dead crawling out of their graves.

"Dance like a skeleton!" Nora shouted.

Letting their arms hang down from their elbows like a pair of scarecrows, Beth and Kellen danced around each other. They were having too good a time to notice the handsome, dark-haired guy who stepped out of the crowd. He was staring at the dancers.

By now, Kellen was into it. He matched Beth move for move. They twisted their arms together and apart like two skeletons trying to find something to hold them up.

The mayor nudged the sheriff and pointed to Beth and Kellen. "Now that's dancing!" he said.

Beth grinned. It was fun to dance like a skeleton. As Kellen danced around her, she turned . . . and caught the gaze of the handsome newcomer.

At that moment, everything—music, the crowd, even Kellen—faded away. Who was this guy? She'd never seen such a drop-dead gorgeous boy before.

Beth forced herself to look away and dance with Kellen, who hadn't noticed anything. Even as she got back into the beat, she was aware that the guy was still watching her . . .

"Now, everyone," said Nora, lifting her arms into the air, "dance like a monster!"

Kellen wasn't sure how a monster danced, but he threw out his arms and bounced from one foot to the other. Beth matched his steps. Everyone on the floor was having fun. Even Luke and Nicole were getting into it.

A distant squeak caught Beth's attention. She looked up to see the weather vane on the gazebo spin. The evening's gentle southern breeze had suddenly changed direction. Now it was a cold north wind.

Beth stared at the weather vane, forgetting to concentrate on the dance. Kellen grabbed her hands and swung them together, thrusting her to her right. But Beth missed her cue. She dropped to the floor and slid toward the boots of a tall, gaunt man in a top hat and an antique black suit. He had a narrow beard and a mustache, and his skin had a faintly grayish hue. His laugh was strange, and his smile reminded her of a cat about to pounce on a mouse.

Beth flinched as thunder shook the pavilion. Lightning flashed, seeming to surround the man in the top hat.

Creepy, she thought.

CHAPTER 4

THE DANCERS STOPPED. THE MUSIC

stopped. And it wasn't on purpose, because the DJ was bending over his setup, trying to see what was wrong. Had it been struck by lightning?

Kellen hurried over to help Beth. When she was back on her feet, she and Kellen noticed that a strikingly beautiful girl had come to stand by the man with the frightening laugh. Her hair was both red and black at the same time. Not streaked, just blended together in shades of blood and night. Her long dress was as black as the man's coat, and she held a stack of papers in her ebony-gloved hands. The girl gave Kellen a half smile, annoying Beth for reasons she couldn't quite explain.

"What a fun festival this is," said the man in the hat. He didn't stop smiling, but it wasn't a smile you wanted to return. "There is plenty more to come. Scary Halloween fun.

"I am Dr. Hysteria, and my Hall of Horrors is not for the faint of heart. But it is for you—if you crave the shake and shiver, the thrill and chill of a fearsome, dark journey into the wretched black heart of pure evil itself."

"But fun," said the girl beside him. Her jet-black necklace caught the light and twinkled as she smiled.

Everyone laughed nervously, breaking the spell of Dr. Hysteria's voice. It was just a show, after all.

"Yessss," Dr. Hysteria said, drawing out the "ess" like a hissing snake. "But fun. Fun for your whole family," he added. "All are welcome to join us. If you dare to walk through the grim, black gates of the Hall of Horrors."

"We open right here tomorrow night," the girl said, spreading her hands wide.

"We close at the stroke of midnight on Halloween." Dr. Hysteria laughed that deep laugh that sent another chill down Beth's spine. "Everything you need to know is on the flyer."

The girl threw her papers high into the air. As the sheets drifted toward the ground, everyone strained to be the first to grab one.

Kellen plucked one out of the air and chuckled when the girl gave him a smile that suggested he'd done a great job catching it.

Dr. Hysteria put a thumb and finger to his mouth and made a sharp whistle. A horse's whinny answered. As he and the girl turned to go, she tossed the rest of the flyers over her shoulder as if she didn't care where they landed. The wind swirled them overhead.

Beth gasped when she saw a coal-black horse heading toward them. It was pulling an open carriage with black velvet seats.

There was no driver.

CHAPTER 5

THE HORSE REARED AND THEN

stopped in front of them. Dr. Hysteria and his assistant climbed into the front seat. He picked up the reins and slapped them on the horse's back. "Hi-yah!" was the last they heard as the pair made their dramatic exit. It was as if Dr. Hysteria wanted to make sure everyone saw them before they left.

Luke grabbed Kellen's shoulder, grinning. "All right. I wanna go! I need to go!"

Beth patted Luke's cheek and smiled. She knew he wanted to go. This was just the kind of thing that Luke—and the rest of them—had hoped would be part of the harvest festival.

She looked at the flyer Kellen held. It was black—no surprise!—and had old-fashioned lettering on it in bright orange and blue. At the top it announced: DR. HYSTERIA'S HALL OF HORRORS. Under the headline was a picture of the man himself, pointing at two yellow ovals by his feet.

Both showed hideous creatures: One was labeled GAR-GOYLES, and the other GHOULS. It gave the dates for three nights that week, closing at midnight on Halloween.

"Admission is just four bucks," Luke said, as if his friends needed convincing. "C'mon. Let's go."

Beth looked at Kellen, and they both smiled.

Half an hour later, Kellen, Beth, Luke, and Nicole were headed toward home. They strolled past houses decked out for Halloween, but Kellen didn't pay them any attention. They'd left the harvest festival shortly after Dr. Hysteria made his appearance. Nothing could top that. Not even the dance contest. Beth and Kellen had won easily. In fact, half the contestants hadn't even bothered to stay until the end. Everyone wanted to talk about Dr. Hysteria and his beautiful assistant. That girl had her role down pat.

But when Kellen looked at Beth, the other girl was forgotten. They were almost to her house, and he still hadn't asked her out. Maybe he just didn't have the nerve.

Walking in the road while his friends took up the sidewalk, Luke began rapping. Kellen laid down the beat.

"I'm strollin' with my posse . . ."

"Yo!" chorused Kellen and Beth.

"'Cause we got the moxie."

"Yo! Yo!"

"Beth and Kellen won the contest . . ."

"Yo! Yo!"

"Why don't you give it a rest?" Nicole jumped in to finish the rhyme. "And what in the world is *moxie?*"

All three of them began laughing and teasing Luke. Kellen and Beth high-fived Nicole.

"Whatever," Luke said. He was peeved that Nicole had stolen his chance for a good punch line. He sighed, but nobody noticed. They'd stopped in front of Beth's house.

As they were saying good-bye, Nicole's phone rang. She scowled. "That's the parents. I've gotta go."

As Beth and Nicole hugged, Luke fist-bumped Kellen. "Tomorrow night. Get our scare on. We will give Dr. Hysteria something to be hysterical about."

"Yes!" Kellen said.

"Good night," Beth added as Luke and Nicole headed toward their own houses.

Kellen didn't move. When Beth turned to say good night, he asked, "Ah . . . later on, you wanna come over for a little bit?" He glanced toward his house, across the street.

Beth looked at her feet. "I really would, but I can't. I've got a lot of homework."

"Oh . . ." He couldn't let her see how disappointed he was. That wouldn't be cool, and Beth deserved a cool guy.

The strong, heroic type. A guy who got bummed because she had to do her homework was no hero.

"You can keep this, if you want," Kellen said, handing her the trophy they'd won at the contest. It was six inches tall, topped by a gold man and woman swirling in a fancy waltz. Nothing like the fun steps they'd made up on the spot.

Beth took it, shooting him a look of mock horror. "Kellen! You would part with this example of fine craftsmanship?" She laughed. "I actually think this is cheaper than my peewee soccer trophy, which I won, I think, for second place."

Kellen laughed. "Hey, we were good together, right?"

"Yeah. We rocked." She turned to leave. "See you in school tomorrow."

He couldn't let the night end. Not yet. "Wait!"

Beth brushed at her coat sleeve. "Ugh! Do I have a bug on me?"

"No, no, no." He took a couple steps toward her. Now or never . . . No, he didn't like the sound of that. He'd have another chance if he blew this one. Wouldn't he? "It's just that I wanted to tell you something."

"Whew," she said, obviously relieved, but he could tell she thought he was teasing her. "Yeah, sure. What's up?"

He closed the distance between them. He swallowed.

Hard. Something was clogging his throat. How was he going to ask her out if he couldn't talk?

Maybe he'd be better off not saying anything. As he looked at her lips and then up to her eyes, she gazed at him. Her eyes widened. Did she know what he was going to do? He wasn't even sure himself. He moved closer, and she didn't move away.

Closer.

Closer.

At the last minute, he lost his nerve. "Remember we've got that—that—that history quiz tomorrow," Kellen blurted. Now he was stuttering on top of acting like a jerk.

Beth looked surprised, and then relieved. That final expression flitting across her face was like a knife through his heart.

"Yeah." She smiled, but it wasn't the same. Everything was weird now. "Thank you." She patted his hand before walking up to the porch. "Bye!" she called over her shoulder.

Kellen watched as she went inside. Then he turned away, groaning inwardly over what a jerk he'd been.

Tomorrow . . . tomorrow morning at school, first thing, he'd ask her to go to the Hall of Horrors with him. He wouldn't chicken out this time. He was going to be the hero he needed to be for such a special girl.

CHAPTER 6

BETH LEANED BACK AGAINST HER front door. What was *that* all about? Kellen had been her best friend since her family had moved to Danville years ago, but he'd been acting so weird lately. He reminded her of Nicole, who pouted if she didn't get her mirror time, and Luke, who wasn't happy unless everyone was laughing over some silly, stupid thing he'd done.

Was she changing, too?

Beth pushed away from the door. She had homework. The big questions of life would have to wait while she studied for her history quiz.

She went into the kitchen and turned on the TV. It was late, so her parents had already gone to bed. The sound from the TV would keep her from drowsing off over the questions about the War of 1812, which seemed to be the most boring war ever.

The news came on, and Beth glanced up, ready for an interruption. It was a reporter outside a suburban house

that didn't look that different from hers. A photo of a girl about her own age appeared on the left side of the screen. Under the picture was the name Andrea Payton, along with a bar that said MISSING GIRL UPDATE.

"The season reminds us that it was Halloween last year when fifteen-year-old Andrea Payton mysteriously disappeared from Federson Township," the reporter said.

The girl's picture filled the screen. She had curly blonde hair.

"She was last seen by friends wearing a maroon Federson High School hoodie and blue jeans," the reporter continued, now with Beth's full attention. "Her family remains hopeful that someone will come forward with information as to her whereabouts. When we return, we'll have all the latest weather updates."

Beth looked down at her homework, but she couldn't help wondering: What had happened to Andrea? A shiver ran down her spine. Federson wasn't far from Danville. It was really kind of freaky that Andrea had just disappeared.

Really freaky.

CHAPTER 7

AT THREE O'CLOCK THE NEXT DAY,
the streets outside Danville High School were busy as
kids and teachers headed for home. Some students walked.
Others drove.

Kellen hurried over to Beth, who was lugging her bag
down the front stairs.

"Hey!" he called.

She stopped. "Hi!"

Kellen grasped the straps of his backpack. Here was
his chance. He'd better take it while he could. "I just want
to tell you—that is—there's something I want to talk
about . . ."

The powerful rumble of a car engine drowned out his
words. He and Beth turned to see a long black muscle car
pull into the school's driveway. The door opened.

Beth drew in a sharp breath. The drop-dead gorgeous
guy she'd seen during the dance contest stepped out. He

was dressed in a gray shirt and black pants, and his black combat boots gave him a cool, bad-boy vibe.

"Do you know who that guy is?" she asked Kellen.

Before he could answer, the guy approached them. "Hey," he said. "You were at that dance contest yesterday. Congratulations." He looked straight at Beth. "You and your boyfriend were great."

"Oh, he's not my boyfriend," Beth said. "We're just buds."

"Cool. I'm Hunter Grey. I just moved here," the guy said.

"I'm Beth, and this is Kellen."

"So Beth, you think I could convince you to go with me to that Hall of Horrors thing?"

Hunter was asking her out when they'd met only a few seconds ago? She giggled. That was the most flattering thing a boy had ever done for her.

"Um . . . okay," she said. She glanced at Kellen, who wasn't smiling.

Beth frowned at him. He was acting weird again.

"In the meantime, can you point me to the office?" Hunter said.

"I can take you," she replied.

"Sweet."

Kellen just stood there, shocked, as Beth and Hunter walked away together.

"Oh, hold up a second," Beth said. She hurried back to where Kellen stood. "Kel, did you want to talk to me about something?"

"Oh . . . uh . . . never mind," he said.

"Okay." She looked back at Hunter.

"All right," said Hunter, smiling at her. They started toward the office again. "Hey," he told Kellen offhandedly, "maybe we'll see you tomorrow, too . . . partner."

It was a low blow, and it burned.

A hand slapped Kellen's arm. It was Luke, hopping from one foot to another. "Kell-man," he said. "Wanna get a smoothie?"

Kellen shook his head, still staring at Beth and Hunter, who were laughing together. "Nah, I'm good."

Luke followed his gaze. "Who's that guy?"

"New kid. His name's Hunter."

"Looks like Hunter's found his prey." When Kellen didn't laugh, Luke frowned. "Dude, what's happened to your sense of humor? All right, I'll see you later, right?"

"Maybe," Kellen said. He sighed, shifted his backpack, and headed for home.

Kellen decided to take the long way, by the fairgrounds where the Hall of Horrors would open tomorrow. A new chain-link fence surrounded the grounds.

Kellen turned away. Now that Beth was going to the

Hall of Horrors with Hunter, he wasn't sure he'd even bother checking it out.

Suddenly, the section of fence next to him rattled loudly.

Kellen whipped around and gasped.

A ghoulish creature on the other side was staring right at him.

CHAPTER 8

KELLEN LOOKED AGAIN. IT WAS JUST a person dressed as a ghoul, emptying a large garbage can. *Probably one of the actors in that dumb Dr. Hysteria show,* Kellen told himself. *What a phony.*

"So," came a voice from behind the ghoul. "Who won the dance contest?"

It was the girl who'd tossed the flyers into the air yesterday. Behind her he could see DR. HYSTERIA'S HALL OF HORRORS painted in huge letters across the front of a large tent. Around it were other smaller tents spreading in every direction.

The main tent's entrance looked like a giant version of Dr. Hysteria's mouth, as if he'd swallow people whole as they entered his haunted house.

"Uh, you mean yesterday?" Kellen asked, realizing the girl was waiting for an answer. "The dance contest. Beth and I won."

"Beth . . ." the girl said, tilting her head. The brilliant purple of her eye shadow made her eyes look even bigger, and her voice was as silky as melted chocolate. "Is she that really pretty girl you were dancing with?"

"Pretty? Yeah, Beth is pretty," he agreed, though at the moment he couldn't take his eyes off *this* girl. Something about her pale skin against her black costume, maybe. Or the way her lipstick was almost the exact shade of red-black as her hair.

"Mm-hmm . . . I noticed this other guy who kept checking her out," the girl went on. "A super-good-looking guy. I mean, like, really good-looking. You could see his muscles through his shirt."

"Yeah, that would be Hunter." Talking about Hunter was the last thing Kellen wanted to do. First Beth, now this girl. He felt like a loser. And it felt even worse when he admitted, "I think she sorta likes him."

"Maybe she's just trying to make you jealous."

He smiled in spite of himself. "No, Beth's not like that. She doesn't play games."

She laughed. When she smiled, she looked more like a high school girl than a carnival performer. "You don't know much about girls, do you? But if you're right, I think your Beth is making the wrong choice."

That made him feel better. He grinned at her.

"I'm Lilith, by the way," she said.

"I'm Kellen."

Lilith smiled in a way that suggested she knew a lot more about him than just his name. Then she took a half step toward the big tent. "Well, Kellen, I gotta get back to work. I hope you come to the show."

Kellen watched her walk to the tent, her black dress swaying above her tall boots. A moment later, she was gone.

Yeah, he'd be back. He wanted to learn more about what was behind that strange doorway . . . and more about Lilith.

CHAPTER 9

UNDER THE LIGHTS THAT CRISS-
crossed the town square, the harvest festival was humming
with activity. Spooky music floated from the end of the
street, where the Hall of Horrors was ablaze with eerie
lights. A large tent with a banner of Dr. Hysteria's face
dominated the block.

Performers dressed as zombies were chained to walls
facing the street, while ghouls wandered through the
crowd. Witches and vampires mingled among those who
dared to venture into the shadows. Kids from five to fifteen squealed with delighted horror.

Popcorn in hand, Mayor Smith strolled along, smiling. Then a ghoul lunged at him. Popcorn flew in every
direction, but the mayor put on a brave face. "Oh, my!
That's really real." He grinned weakly before hurrying in
the opposite direction.

"Our fearless leader," Luke said, hooking a thumb at
the mayor. He and Kellen were headed toward the Hall of

Horrors. Luke was grinning, ready to have a good time, but Kellen wasn't paying him any attention. He was searching for Beth. She and her new friend Hunter should have been here by now.

"This place is so awesome. Do you think they sell churros?"

"You and your churros, man," Kellen said.

Luke began one of his raps—

"I like a churro.
Lights up my neuro.
Got one at home, yo.
In my bureau."

Kellen shook his head. Usually Luke's dumb raps made him laugh, but tonight, he had other things on his mind. Where was Beth?

A group of ten-year-old girls posing for a photo suddenly screamed and rushed past Kellen and Luke. An actor dressed as a witch was chasing them.

Everyone laughed, but Luke said seriously, "Now remember, this is all makeup and special effects." But when another witch jumped out and hissed at him, he nearly jumped into Kellen's arms.

Even that didn't make Kellen laugh. He couldn't stop thinking about Beth and Hunter.

"Hey, guys," Nicole called, making her way toward them.

"Nicole!" Luke cried. "Look out!" He pulled her out of the way of a goblin who'd been sneaking up behind her.

"Back off, wormface," he told the goblin. "Don't be messin' with my lady."

The goblin slunk away. Nicole smiled up at Luke.

Kellen was still scanning the crowd, which was much thicker near the entrance to the Hall of Horrors.

"We should go in together," Nicole said with a nervous laugh.

Kellen didn't notice. He'd finally seen Beth. She and Hunter had tickets in their hands.

"Hey," Beth greeted them.

"Hey, everyone," Hunter added. "This is great, huh? I love all these costumes."

"Ooooh, look at that one." Beth pointed at a chained zombie who was trying to grab visitors as they walked by.

Luke couldn't wait any longer. "I'll get the tickets." He hurried to the ticket booth.

A familiar voice caught Kellen's attention. Lilith! She stood in the middle of the street, calling out to the crowd. "Do not feed the zombies. Beware of the ghouls. Do not look the witches in the eye."

As Beth and Hunter headed toward the entrance,

Kellen made straight for Lilith. He put up one hand as if to shield his eyes.

"What are you doing?" she asked.

"You said not to look the witches in the eye."

She laughed. "Don't worry. I'm not a witch. I'm an enchantress."

He lowered his hand. "Then I should definitely look away."

"If you can." Lilith smiled and raised her eyebrows at him. Then she repeated her chant. "Do not feed the zombies. Beware of the ghouls. Do NOT look the witches in the eye."

Kellen went to catch up with his friends, but couldn't help glancing back at Lilith. There was something strange but interesting about her.

He was still thinking of her as he walked into the Hall of Horrors. He'd forgotten all about Beth. For a moment, he was too preoccupied with Lilith and her amazing eyes.

CHAPTER 10

BETH HANDED OVER HER TICKET
and held out her hand. A ghoul stamped it with a picture
of Dr. Hysteria. His eyes seemed to be looking directly
at her.

It's just a stamp, she told herself. But it was creepy.

She joined her friends, and they walked into the Hall
of Horrors together. Behind them, a wall of steam separated them from the crowds waiting to get in.

Beth led Hunter, Luke, Kellen, and Nicole as they
wended their way through a maze of corridors. There
were colored lights, but mist clouded everything.

The deeper the kids moved into the maze, the creep-
ier the sounds that echoed around them. Screams. Moans.
Creaking doors. Spooky noises seemed to come from
everywhere and nowhere.

Along the maze's walls, jutting out into the narrow
pathways, were skulls and coffins. Candles flickered and

went out before mysteriously lighting again. The air was thick with smoke and the smell of mildew.

Beth drew in her arms, not wanting to touch anything. Even though she knew it was just a show, her heart pounded against her chest. Breathing wasn't easy, because she knew if she took a deep breath, it would come out as a scream.

Suddenly, Beth regretted going first. But she couldn't step back now and let someone else take the lead.

As they passed a corpse playing a pipe organ, another jumped out at her with a screech. Beth shrank away from it, almost bumping into Hunter, who seemed to be taking everything in stride. He put his hands on her shoulders as he followed her farther into the Hall of Horrors.

"Kellen, I don't want to do this," Nicole moaned.

"You'll be fine," Beth said, and then screamed as a goblin leered at her from the shadows. Beth laughed along with everyone else, but the place really wasn't her idea of fun.

Next, they passed Count Dracula and more ghouls. As one leaped out of a side room, the visitors had to slip past single file.

Luke offered Nicole to Dracula. "Take her. Take her."

Nicole didn't bother laughing. She just glowered at him.

Another door loomed before them. Beth took a hesitant step in. There was a coffin in the center of the room.

Suddenly, the lid flew open, and a rotting, ragged zombie leaped out. "Quiet down!" he ordered. "I'm trying to sleep." He sank out of sight, and the lid slammed shut again.

Everyone giggled, but their laughter was short-lived. A banshee was swooping overhead, screeching and reaching for their hair.

Nicole threw her arms around Kellen, hiding her face against his chest.

"Hey, Kellen, I didn't know your mom worked here," Luke cracked.

Nicole whirled around. "Will you just cool it?"

They followed Beth down a dim, narrow hallway. In the dark, Beth nearly crashed into a ghoul wearing a dusty black karate gi. Behind her, lightning flashed and thunder rumbled. The odor of smoke was suffocating.

Suddenly, Dr. Hysteria appeared high above their heads. It turned out to be a hologram, but there was something about his leering, flickering image that was even scarier than the man himself.

"Honored guests . . . or should I say, unfortunate victims?" He laughed wickedly at his own joke. "I invite you on a journey to . . . Zombie Boulevard." He gave another evil laugh . . . and then vanished.

Beth smiled in nervous anticipation as a ghoul drew aside a velvet rope and let them pass. Terrifying sights

awaited them on the other side. A mother zombie was feeding a baby zombie. The bottle appeared to be filled with blood. Other zombies jumped out of the darkness, growling.

Beth screamed, then covered her mouth with her hands. It was so real! She looked back. Nicole was clinging to Kellen's arm. Whenever something moved, she pressed her face to his shoulder.

Kellen was laughing. His calm reaction gave Beth a second wind, and she continued on.

When they turned another corner, an undead vendor was holding up an enormous fork with a desiccated hot dog on the end.

"Brains on a stick!" it called. "Get your brains on a stick!"

Chuckling, Beth eased by him, making sure not to touch any of his wares. She jumped aside as a zombie nurse reached long-nailed fingers toward her. She felt better when Hunter stepped around her to take the lead.

They entered a schoolroom. A zombie teacher was standing at the front, teaching three undead children.

The students intoned in halting voices, "A . . . G . . . Z . . . B . . ."

"Perrr-fffect," said the zombie teacher.

"Guess now we know why zombies are always looking for brains," Luke said.

Beth giggled. It was funny and creepy at the same time. She kept both hands around Hunter's arm. But her laughter broke off when Hunter put his hand over hers, giving it a squeeze, before he led the way out of the room.

Kellen pushed his way to her side, between her and Hunter. "Cool show, right?" he said.

"Yes. Totally." She was suddenly uneasy. She could tell Hunter made Kellen uncomfortable.

As a few other kids passed by, he asked, "Can I talk to you for a sec?" He glanced at Hunter. "Alone?"

She was surprised when Hunter said, "I'll just go on ahead. Okay?"

"You don't have to—"

"It's okay," Hunter said.

As Hunter continued down a corridor illuminated by a flashing strobe light, Beth took a deep breath. Why did Kellen have to talk to her *now*? What was so important it couldn't wait until after they were done with the Hall of Horrors? "What's up, Kellen?"

"Nothing . . ." Even in the dark, she could see that his face was serious, maybe even sad. "I mean . . . so . . . you and Hunter . . ."

"What?"

"You're like . . ."

"We're like what?"

Kellen flung out his hands, almost hitting a kid passing by. "I don't know . . . you know . . . I mean . . . I see you guys are, like, holding hands."

"Kellen, were you watching us through binoculars or something?"

He shook his head. "No, I . . . um . . . it's all good . . ."

"Okay," she said, relieved.

"I'm just . . ." He squared his shoulders. "You know, never mind." He stepped around her and followed their friends down the corridor.

She watched him go. Kellen wasn't acting like himself at all. In fact, he hadn't been acting like himself since the dance contest.

"Brains on a stick!" snarled the zombie, thrusting a skewer close to her face.

She cringed until the zombie moved away.

The lights dimmed. She couldn't see anything. Or hear anyone. Where were Hunter and Kellen and Nicole and Luke?

To her right, a door slowly creaked open, letting in a finger of light.

"Hello?" Beth called. "Where is everybody?"

As lights flashed and terrible screams sounded in the distance, Beth hurried to the door and pushed it open wider. She wanted out of this place. It wasn't fun by herself.

And whatever was on the other side of the door couldn't possibly be worse than what was on this side.

Could it?

She stepped through a dimly lit corridor. Curtains covered several walls. Were there rooms behind them? She wasn't in the mood to explore. She wanted to find her friends and get out of here.

Beth strode down the corridor, her boots echoing on the floor. She shouldn't be here. She knew that, and she didn't want to get caught. But going back wasn't an option. She'd had enough of the Hall of Horrors.

As she turned a corner, she heard a curtain pulled shut behind her. A rat raced across the floor. *Just an effect*, she told herself . . . but it looked real.

A door slammed. Beth heard loud footsteps headed her way. They were getting louder and louder.

She wasn't alone anymore.

CHAPTER 11

"did you LEAVE THIS dOOR OPEN?" A snarling voice asked.

Beth was hidden behind a curtain. She peeked out to see a vampire in an elegant opera cape and tuxedo confronting a zombie in a dress shirt and tie.

"Uhhhh . . ." the zombie said.

"What if someone saw it?" demanded the vampire, his fangs glistening in the weak light.

The zombie mumbled again.

"Idiot!" With a whirl of his cloak, the vampire pushed aside the curtain and disappeared through the doorway beyond it. The zombie followed him with a lurch.

Beth waited until she was sure they were gone. Then she ran back to the door and tugged on the knob. It was locked!

She looked both ways. What next?

Beth took a deep breath, trying to calm herself. Those ghouls and vampires were just actors, right? She'd stumbled backstage, and now all she had to do was walk back out again. The actors might yell at her for poking her nose where it didn't belong, but then they'd lead her out of the Hall of Horrors.

Out! That's all she wanted. To get out of this place, find her friends, and never come back again.

Drawing aside the curtain, Beth slipped into the room where she'd seen the zombie and vampire. It was obviously a dressing room for the actors. She'd find one of them, and . . .

She passed a rack of clothing and then stopped and stared. The vampire sat by a makeup mirror, sharpening his fangs with a file.

Beth glanced in the mirror. There was her reflection. But the vampire didn't have one!

She swallowed a scream. Everyone knew that vampires don't have reflections. But that was just in books and movies.

Beth looked again. All she saw was her terrified face.

The vampire looked up from his fangs and spotted her pale face in the mirror. As he spun to face her, his expression tightened into a hideous glare. He made a horrible threatening sound, half roar and half hiss.

Beth turned and ran.

She heard the vampire call to the zombie to join him. They were going to catch her! She ran faster.

There had to be a way out somewhere. But where?

Behind her, their footsteps were drawing closer. Beth hid behind a pole and spotted more racks of costumes. Desperately, she pushed her way through the clothing. There had to be a place to hide—or even better, a way out!

There was no exit in sight. So Beth squatted on the floor, wishing she were invisible.

She heard sniffing. Like a dog trailing someone.

"Flesh," growled the zombie.

He came closer and closer, sniffing.

"Flesh?" He sounded less sure.

He drew closer still, sniffing the air and lurching heavily from side to side. Then he moved away.

Beth closed her eyes and drew in a silent breath.

A hand, mottled and rotting, suddenly pushed between the clothes, just inches from her face. She bit back a scream.

"Flesh . . ." the zombie moaned.

CHAPTER 12

BETH FROZE. HER EYES DARTED

about, looking for an escape, any escape from this horror.

A rat ran right by her foot. She saw the zombie's hand, his fingers spread wide, searching the clothing again. He was closer this time.

A rat! Beth felt paralyzed by fear. If only this was all a bad dream.

But she knew that it was no dream. She had to do something or the zombie would devour her.

Gritting her teeth, Beth grabbed the rat and thrust it into the zombie's open hand.

His fingers closed around it. A moment later, he'd pulled it back through the racks of clothes. "Flesh." There was triumph in his voice.

He stood up, bringing the rat to his lips. He licked it slowly, and then stuffed it into his mouth and began chewing.

Behind him, the vampire muttered something about zombies and their appalling diets. He turned and began pacing on the other side of the room.

While they were both distracted, Beth grabbed a black cloak from the end of the costume rack. This was her chance.

This time, she didn't hesitate. She draped the black cloak over her head and slipped into the shadows and out of the room.

What she'd seen was no act. She would have to try to make sense of it later. Right now, all she wanted was to get out of the Hall of Horrors while she still could.

Beth took steady steps as she walked down the hall. She tried to look as though she belonged there. She didn't want to stand out in any way. She continued down the corridor and around the corner. She didn't stop when she saw a ghoul and a gremlin coming toward her. She prepared to run if they stopped her.

But they didn't. They walked past her as if she didn't exist.

Beth hurried around another corner, hoping to find an unlocked door. But she was starting to feel as though she were back in the maze. She kept turning corner after corner with no exit in sight. She had to figure out which turns to take and which turns led to traps.

As she turned another corner, she saw blue strobe lights flickering ahead of her. A freak with a chainsaw

stood on a bed. Beth froze as he swung the chainsaw. Was he coming after her?

Meanwhile, Kellen, Nicole, and Luke had made it almost all of the way through the Hall of Horrors.

Nicole spotted Hunter coming around the corner. He actually looked a little bored.

Luke grabbed hold of Kellen at the same time Nicole did. A portrait of Dr. Hysteria hung on the wall before them—but the moment they looked at it, the portrait vanished! The three kids screamed as the real Dr. Hysteria materialized where the painting once stood.

"Good night!" their ghoulish host said. "Come back soon for more scary fun. Sleep with one eye open."

Dr. Hysteria disappeared as suddenly as he'd appeared, and the painting reappeared in his place.

Kellen pulled Nicole, Luke, and Hunter out of the Hall of Horrors.

Back on the street, Mayor Smith was bouncing from one foot to the other. "Sweet pumpkin fritters!" he exclaimed with an uneasy laugh. His hair stood on end. He hurried over to his wife and children. "That is kind of fun, huh, kids? Wow! That felt really real! Hey, you know it looked like I was crying, but I was just pretending. I wasn't really crying."

His wife patted his arm with a knowing smile.

"That was awesome," Luke said, savoring the moment. "Nicole, you screamed about seven times."

Nicole noticed Kellen's troubled face. He was looking up and down the street. "Are you okay?"

He turned to her and shrugged. "Me? Yeah, I'm fine."

"Me?" Luke said. "I'm starving." He wandered over to the closest food booth.

"We should get something to eat," Nicole said, more to Kellen than to Luke.

"No, you go," Kellen said as he kept scanning the crowd. "I think I'm gonna take off."

Nicole grabbed his arm. "Kellen, Beth's not the only girl in world, you know."

"No, no, I . . . I just feel like going for a walk." He turned and walked away.

Nicole watched him for a moment. Then she sighed and joined Luke by the food truck. He always made her laugh.

Back in the Hall of Horrors, Beth had spotted a door labeled VIP. It opened onto the street. Beth was so surprised and relieved, she practically tumbled out. People stared at her, and she wondered if her terror showed on her face. Then she remembered she was still wearing the black cloak. She pulled it off, balled it up, and left it by the door. Then she took off. She wanted to get as far away from this place as possible.

On the other side of the big tent, she saw a welcome face. "Hey, Hunter," she said, hurrying over to him. "I'm so glad I found you."

Behind her, Dr. Hysteria emerged from a side entrance to the Hall of Horrors. He stared across the street at Beth and Hunter. His face was blank. There was no ghoulish humor, no challenging invitation to the Hall of Horrors. He just watched in silence as Beth and Hunter walked away.

Beth turned when she felt his eyes on her. Hunter was trying to calm her down, but a chill went down her spine when she spotted Dr. Hysteria.

A slow, satisfied smile inched across his face.

Later, back at home, Beth sat at her desk and opened her laptop. She had every light in the room on, including the purple Christmas lights wrapped around her canopy bed.

She had to know what was going on. As fast as she could, she searched for *Dr. Hysteria's Hall of Horrors*.

A page of links popped up. The first link led to reviews of the show. She began to look through them, reading each one.

She wasn't sure what she expected to find, but she knew what she was looking for: the truth about what was really going on there.

Eventually, she clicked a link that led to a schedule of the show's events. She glanced down at today's date, but it was the wrong day of the week—the schedule was a day off.

It was last year's calendar.

She looked up at the top of the page and read *Federson Chamber of Commerce*.

Federson!

She remembered the news report: *Andrea Payton mysteriously disappeared from Federson Township.*

On Halloween!

There had to be a connection.

What was really going on in Dr. Hysteria's Hall of Horrors?

CHAPTER 13

KELLEN TRUDGED TOWARD HOME. HE had his headphones on, and he was trying to lose himself in the music. All he wanted was to forget tonight and everything that had happened. He'd meant for this to be a fun night for him and Beth. How had it all gone so wrong? Beth had gone off with Hunter like he wasn't even there.

At least the street was empty, so he didn't have to pretend to be polite to anyone he passed. It was late, and some of the houses were dark. That made the Halloween decorations even spookier.

A single headlight made its way down the middle of the street. Kellen didn't notice anything unusual until a motorcycle stopped beside him.

He tipped back his headphones as the rider tipped back her helmet, revealing a girl with green eyes.

It was Lilith, but not the Lilith he'd seen before. In the glow from the streetlight, he could see she was wearing a black leather jacket and jeans and had normal makeup on. She looked even prettier than usual. She didn't need all that makeup she wore for the show.

"Hi," she said.

"Oh, it's you. I didn't . . ."

"Recognize me out of costume?" She held up her hands. "This is the real me. I like to drive around after the show." She leaned one arm on the bike's handlebar. "Just to chill out, y'know?"

He nodded, fascinated by the change in her. Only her silky voice and amazing eyes were the same.

"I saw you wandering around aimlessly," Lilith went on. "I thought one of our zombies had escaped."

"Sorry to disappoint you." He grinned. He liked this version of Lilith.

She eyed him up and down. "You didn't."

"So what's it like?"

"Working in the show?"

He nodded.

"I love it," she said. "I was born into it, but *you* would be great in it."

"Me?" Kellen laughed at the idea. He couldn't imagine himself leaping out of shadows and frightening people. He couldn't even get up the nerve to ask a girl to go to the movies with him.

"Why not? Most of our performers started working with us when they were about your age. And I started when I was a little girl."

"Yeah, well, I don't think I'm the show-business type."

"Are you sure?" she asked, teasing now. "I've seen your wicked dance moves."

"That was all Beth."

"You've got style—your own style. Don't let anyone tell you otherwise." She picked up a second helmet off the back of the bike and held it out to him. "I'll take you home." When he hesitated, she said, "It's not on fire. Get on."

He took the helmet and straddled the back of the motorcycle. Pulling on the helmet, he put his hands on either side of her narrow waist.

"Wrap 'em around," she said.

He did, and she revved the motorcycle. A moment later, they were zooming down the street.

Back in her room, Beth was still researching Dr. Hysteria. She looked up when she heard an engine start. Was that a motorcycle?

She switched off her lights, went to the window, lifted one slat of the blinds, and looked out.

A motorcycle with two riders stopped across the street, in front of Kellen's house. The rider on the back took off his helmet and climbed off.

It was Kellen.

With Dr. Hysteria's gorgeous assistant.

What were they doing out on a motorcycle so late at night? No, wait; Beth didn't want an answer to that question. She should drop the slat and walk away.

But she couldn't. She watched as if she were witnessing a horrible accident. The girl grabbed Kellen's coat and pulled him toward her until they were cheek-to-cheek. Was she whispering something to him?

When Kellen leaned back away from her, he stumbled a couple of steps before regaining his balance. He watched as the girl drove away.

And Beth saw a lipstick mark on his cheek.

Dr. Hysteria's assistant had kissed him.

Kellen glanced up at Beth's house just as she closed the blind.

Beth shook her head. She felt strange. It was a shock. She didn't want Kellen mixed up with anyone from that show. Not when she had so many questions.

That was the reason she was upset about the kiss. It didn't have anything to do with how she felt about Kellen. He was her friend, her buddy, her partner.

Right?

Beth went into the bathroom and filled the sink. Her mind was racing with questions, but she was exhausted. Things would be clearer in the morning.

She looked at the stamp on her hand. It hadn't faded or smudged. She dunked her hand in the water and scrubbed at it. She didn't want anything to do with Dr. Hysteria and whatever was going on there.

Lifting her hand out of the water, she looked at it. The stamp was just the same.

Odd . . .

She washed it again, harder this time.

It was still there.

Maybe three times was the charm. She scoured her hand again, and then bent over the sink to wash her face. Straightening, she looked in the mirror.

Dr. Hysteria was standing right behind her.

High school friends Kellen, Luke, Beth, and Nicole can't wait to visit Dr. Hysteria's Hall of Horrors, a traveling haunted house that comes to their small town.

Dr. Hysteria and his assistant, Lilith, have a strange hold over the kids.

Beth and Kellen have been best friends forever, but Kellen wishes they could be more.

But then Beth meets Hunter, and Kellen's sure he lost his chance.

Beth and Hunter visit the Hall of Horrors together. But Beth gets lost . . . and discovers some very sinister things.

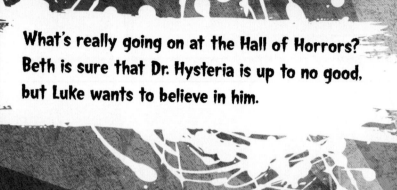

What's really going on at the Hall of Horrors? Beth is sure that Dr. Hysteria is up to no good, but Luke wants to believe in him.

Luke and Nicole are no longer themselves — they've turned into demons!

Beth is the only one able to resist the lure of the Hall of Horrors. Can she save her friends?

CHAPTER 14

dR. HYSTERIA SMIRKEd At BETH IN
the mirror. His look said that he knew more than she ever could.

Beth whirled around. Nobody was there.

What was going on?

Beth wasn't sure of anything. Except that whatever was going on, it wasn't anything good.

The next morning was chilly and gray, but Kellen had a bounce in his step as he cut across the school parking lot. He still couldn't believe that Lilith had given him a ride on her motorcycle. And the kiss . . . *that* was a surprise.

Plus, he'd realized Beth had been watching. She must have seen the kiss. He grinned at the memory. All in all, it hadn't been a bad night.

"Kellen!"

Beth was rushing to catch up with him. He stopped by the front door.

"Hey!" she said. "Can I talk to you?"

He nodded, and they walked into school together. Beth quickly filled him in on what had happened to her after she'd been separated from the rest of the group. It grew weirder and weirder with every word. But then, everything about Dr. Hysteria's show was weird. Didn't Beth realize that? He didn't want to say so, though, because he could see that however crazy it sounded, she believed what she was saying.

When Beth paused to take a breath, Kellen asked, "You saw the zombie *eat* a live rat?"

"No! I didn't see it, but I heard it."

"And you saw a real vampire?"

"Yes! He was real, because I was right in front of the mirror. And he had no reflection."

"C'mon, Beth," he said. "It's supposed to be a haunted house. It's full of trick mirrors."

"What about the missing girl? Andrea Payton went missing from Federson Township the *exact same week* the Hall of Horrors was there."

"That doesn't prove anything. Why are you so worried about the Hall of Horrors? I'll say it again. It's just a show."

"What about this?" She raised her hand and pointed at the Dr. Hysteria stamp. "Have you tried washing off the stamp on your hand?"

He glanced at his hand. The stamp was still there. "I mean . . . I just took a shower. I didn't scrub it."

"Mine won't come off no matter how much I scrub it . . ."

"So? It's strong ink." Kellen didn't have time for anything else, because Hunter was coming toward them.

"Hi!" Hunter put his arm around Beth's shoulders. "Is he going to help us?"

"Us?" asked Kellen, though he already knew what Hunter was going to say next.

"Yeah, Beth thinks there's something weird about the Hall of Horrors," Hunter said.

Kellen shrugged. "Good luck with that."

Hunter nodded. "We'll find out. You'll see."

Beth smiled up at Hunter like they were the only two people in the world.

"Looks like he's got you covered," Kellen told Beth. He turned and walked away.

Yet again, he'd had his chance to step up and be Beth's hero. And yet again, he'd blown it. Would he ever get another chance?

CHAPTER 15

THE LAST LIGHT OF THE DAY WAS

fading away, and a full moon emerged from behind the clouds. Dr. Hysteria glanced at his watch. It was time.

A big crowd was waiting to enter the Hall of Horrors. He smiled as he threw a switch. Electricity sizzled.

Outside, the lights came on, and the music swelled. The crowd cheered. Their wait was over. Dr. Hysteria watched as they pushed and shoved to enter the Hall of Horrors.

Kellen was at home. This time, he was the one to peek through his blinds at Beth's house. He had a great view of Hunter's black car parked out front. As he watched, Beth came out to meet Hunter. She got in the car, and they drove away.

Kellen snapped the blinds shut and turned away in disgust. Was he mad at Beth, or himself? He wasn't sure.

Putting on his headphones, he dropped onto his bed and closed his eyes. A few minutes later, he sat up and plucked at the strings of his guitar. He would try everything he could think of to stop thinking about Beth and Hunter. So far, nothing had worked.

His phone jangled. Kellen glanced at the screen. Luke.

"Hey," Kellen said, wanting to be left alone with his misery.

"Dude, where are you?" Luke demanded.

"Nowhere. Just home."

"Get over here."

He didn't have to ask where *here* was. He could hear the Hall of Horrors' shivery music in the background.

"Naw," he told Luke. "I'm just gonna chill."

Luke's voice took on an edge. "Man! This is all about Beth, isn't it?"

"No," he lied with a fake laugh. "No, it's not."

"I'm looking at them right now. Wow, I think they're kissing!"

"Really?"

"Gotcha!" Luke laughed.

"You're so not funny. I'm serious, dude. It gets old, know what I mean?"

"Fine," Luke replied. "Just fooling with you. But whatever."

The next sound Luke heard was a *beep* as Kellen hung up the phone.

Luke couldn't believe his best friend had just hung up on him. Maybe they'd been cut off. "Hello? Hello?" Turning off his own phone, he mumbled, "Fine. Whatever. Have a nice night."

He spotted a churro vendor wheeling his cart around the side of one of the tents. "Yo, churro!" He trotted after the man. "Hey! Hey! Customer here."

The vendor stopped and faced him. It was Dr. Hysteria.

"Whoa!" Luke said, startled. "Are you a one-man show? So you run the place and you sell churros? You probably sweep up, too, right?"

Dr. Hysteria laughed and handed him a churro. "On the house."

"All right! Thanks." Luke took a bite.

"Are you all by yourself this evening?" the showman asked.

Luke answered with his mouth full. "Yeah. I guess so."

"And where might all your friends be?"

"Well, we kinda had—"

"Had a falling out?" asked Dr. Hysteria.

Luke nodded.

Dr. Hysteria walked back toward the street. "Come with me." He dropped his arm around Luke's shoulders like they were best buddies. "You can bring the churro."

"Where are we going?" Luke asked.

Dr. Hysteria nodded to a door marked VIP ENTRANCE. "You are a very important person," he said.

"I am?" Luke said.

"You are to me," Dr. Hysteria said, leading him through the door. They headed down a long, dim hallway. Bloodred curtains hung over doorways, but they didn't stop at any of them.

"I've been watching you," Dr. Hysteria went on.

"You have?"

"You're funny," Dr. Hysteria said. "But your friends don't laugh. They don't appreciate you. It's because they're jealous. Yesterday, you made a joke when the banshee flew overhead. You said, 'I didn't know your mom worked here.'" He waved a hand. "It's not funny when I say it."

"It was just one of those 'yo mama' jokes."

"You're far too modest." Dr. Hysteria stopped in front of a dark curtain.

Luke looked around. Next to the curtain was a bright yellow sign with big red lettering: DR. HYSTERIA'S MAGIC THEATER. Below was a picture of Dr. Hysteria.

Dr. Hysteria pushed back the curtain and gestured for Luke to enter. Inside was a small theater with four rows of folding chairs. Down in front, there was a stage edged with fancy blue and yellow designs.

"It may be just one of those 'yo mama' jokes," Dr. Hysteria said as they walked to the center aisle, "but it's the way you say it that makes it funny. Your delivery. Say it."

Luke looked at him, unsure. He couldn't remember the last time someone had asked him to do one of his jokes *again*.

"Yo, Kellen, I didn't know your mom worked here," he said.

Dr. Hysteria laughed. "I love the 'yo, Kellen.' Do it again." His face became very serious. "The whole thing."

"Yo, Kellen," Luke said, getting into it big-time, "I didn't know your mom worked here."

Laughter came from the stage.

Lightning seemed to flash across the curtain. The light swirled wider and wider. Luke looked across the theater, where a vision of himself in the future appeared. He was doing stand-up comedy onstage in front of a cheering audience. They were laughing themselves silly. A hip-hop beat played in the background, and Luke began to rap.

"I'll get big yuks and megabucks
To pay me my money gonna need dump trucks
I can do slapstick, I can be pretty
Can make a face . . . Don't need to be witty."

"Very entertaining," said Dr. Hysteria appreciatively.

Luke's smile grew wider and wider as his stage double went on:

"I got my clown on, no frown on
That's no sass—'cause I get laughs like matter gets mass."

Luke laughed, impressed with himself.

"Very clever," added Dr. Hysteria.

"I got more jokes than a forest got trees . . ."

Beside him, Dr. Hysteria's eyes narrowed. But Luke didn't notice. He was totally lost in the lines that seemed to just flow from him. He loved being onstage.

Lightning flashed again. This time, it felt like it was right in Luke's eyes . . .

Everything faded in front of him, and Luke sagged, suddenly feeling drained. He blinked. The stage was empty. He could no longer see himself as a great comedian. He shook his head. His brain seemed to be stuck in neutral.

Beside him, Dr. Hysteria watched him closely.

"Where am I?" muttered Luke.

Dr. Hysteria's voice echoed all around him. "You seem to have wandered through an exit door."

"I don't remember."

"Let me show you out." He motioned toward the curtain at the back of the theater.

Luke nodded, but something was different about him. About Dr. Hysteria. About everything.

He had no idea what it was. But something told him he was in trouble. Serious, dangerous trouble . . .

CHAPTER 16

KELLEN STARED DOWN AT THE PHOTO

on his phone. It was one of his favorite pictures of Beth, taken back when he believed they could become more than just friends. She was laughing, her head thrown back, her blonde hair falling over her shoulders.

He swiped to the next photo. Beth making a goofy face. He laughed in spite of himself. She could always make him laugh when he was feeling lousy.

The next photo was of him and Beth with Nicole and Luke. The four of them were gathered around a birthday cake. Beth was about to blow out the candles. He zoomed in on Beth. She looked so happy . . . just as she had looked when Hunter told her he wanted to help her find out what was going on with Dr. Hysteria's stupid show.

Kellen had messed up everything.

A message popped up on the screen. It was from Nicole. **Where is everyone?**

He texted back. **I'm staying home. Luke's at show.**

A moment passed, and then there was another text from Nicole.

You should come.

He sighed. He didn't want to be with Nicole tonight. It wasn't her fault. He just wanted to be with Beth.

I'm not feeling it. Have fun.

He put his phone down and sighed. Could this night get any worse?

Nicole bit her lower lip. She really didn't want to be here all by herself.

"Kellen should pay attention to you," said a deep voice behind her.

Nicole whirled around. It was Dr. Hysteria. Had he been reading over her shoulder? Why would he do that?

"You know Kellen?" she asked cautiously.

"Young lady, tonight I shall give you a special treat." With a dramatic flourish, he pointed to a door marked VIP.

"The VIP entrance?" That sounded cool to Nicole.

He gave a half bow. "Anything less would be an insult. Don't you think you are a *very important person*?"

Nicole liked the sound of that: a very important person.

Dr. Hysteria took a step toward the door and motioned for her to follow.

Nicole walked through the door. Dr. Hysteria led her to the same magic theater he'd shown Luke. He threw aside the curtain. "After you."

She entered, and immediately a lightning bolt sped across the stage. The light was so bright Nicole couldn't see anything at first. Then she gasped.

To her amazement, she saw herself sitting on a throne. She was dressed in a magnificent gown and golden jewelry. A servant was fixing her hair, which looked perfect already. Classical music played in the background as she picked a grape out of a bowl beside her.

"Fetch my manservant!" she ordered.

A maid quickly left and returned with Kellen, who was wearing a ragged vest and loose trousers. He was barefoot . . . and clearly no match for Queen Nicole.

A small smile crossed the real Nicole's face. She didn't notice that Dr. Hysteria was smiling, too. She was too wrapped up in the fantasy to see anything but Kellen bowing before her.

"How may I serve you, my darling?" he asked, going down on one knee.

"Wow!" the real Nicole murmured. This was even better than anything she'd ever imagined.

Queen Nicole leaned forward as one of her maids sprayed perfume on her glorious hair. She turned to Kellen and said, "My feet are tired."

"Allow me."

Kellen got on his hands and knees in front of her. She raised one foot and then the other onto his back. He was now her footstool.

"Mmm . . ." she hummed in satisfaction.

The real Nicole continued to watch, her smile widening. There was another flash of lightning, blinding her momentarily.

The scene vanished, and Nicole blinked. Where was she? What had happened?

Dr. Hysteria looked on with a knowing smirk.

Nicole walked back onto the street, feeling a bit lost. Something was different . . . but what?

Suddenly, she heard a ghostly voice saying her name. Nicole looked around, but there was no one there.

Then it came again. Her name. It seemed to be coming from the stamp on her hand. The Dr. Hysteria stamp.

"Nicole," she heard, "now you are mine."

She stared down at her hand, confused.

Outside the tent, the chained zombie leaped toward her with a growl.

Nicole quickly backed away, bumping into Luke. He was staring up at the sky as if he had never seen it before.

They looked at each other, said nothing, and walked off in opposite directions.

There was something different . . . about everything.

CHAPTER 17

INSIDE THE HALL OF HORRORS, BETH
heard screams coming from every direction. *Just like last night*, she thought.

Creatures leaped out at the visitors. Just like last night.

Friends joked and jostled and pretended they weren't scared. Just like last night.

But for Beth, nothing was like last night . . .

With Hunter at her side, she made her way through the maze of hallways. She paid no attention to the ghouls and zombies and goblins. She was looking for the door. The special door she'd wandered through last night. She knew it was just past Zombie Boulevard.

As a zombie chased frightened kids through a curtain, Beth turned and spotted the door. She tested the knob. It turned.

She motioned for Hunter to come with her, and they slipped through the door and peered down the dimly lit corridor.

"What exactly are we looking for?" Hunter whispered.

"I'm not sure. I just know that there's something they don't want us to see." She took a deep breath. "Let's go."

She hurried down the corridor with Hunter at her heels. They wandered through a maze that seemed as large as the Hall of Horrors itself. The walls were covered with red silk wallpaper and pictures of people she didn't recognize.

"Gotta say," Hunter murmured, "this is one of the weirdest dates I've ever been on."

She smiled at him. Tonight was high on her weird-o-meter, too.

He grinned back. "I'm not complaining."

When she heard faint moans, Beth put out her hand to halt Hunter. "Do you hear that?"

"Yeah," he said. They continued through the maze, more cautiously now.

They went around a corner. In front of them was a black door. It was the first door she'd seen since they'd left the crowds behind. She glanced at Hunter. The moans were definitely coming from behind the door. What would they find on the other side?

She reached out and turned the handle.

The large room held only one thing. A cabinet. It was about eight feet tall and had a double set of doors covered with carved symbols she couldn't identify. "Oh . . ." said

Hunter. "It's pretty creepy. Probably a prop for one of their shows." He didn't sound very sure.

"Maybe this is what we're not supposed to see," Beth said.

The moans were definitely coming from the cabinet. As she moved closer, she noticed there were words carved at the top. "The Cabinet of Souls," she read aloud.

Another moan came from the cabinet.

"Yeah," Hunter said with a gulp. "Isn't there a saying? You know . . . never open a cabinet of souls in a hall of horrors?"

She shook her head. "I don't think there's a saying."

"There should be."

Strange sounds came from the cabinet. Beth hesitated long enough to look at Hunter, and then reached out to open the doors.

She stared in disbelief. The inside of the cabinet was much deeper than she'd thought. Fog curled up from the floor and fell in a curtain over a stone-edged doorway at the back. Between Beth and the other doorway, two rows of people stood in the silvery-gray light. None of them moved.

When she looked back at Hunter, he shook his head. He wasn't going in there.

But Beth's curiosity refused to let her turn and run. Instead, she stepped around the cabinet. It was only about eighteen inches deep. It made no sense! The cabinet was much deeper than that on the inside. What did it mean?

Beth took a deep breath and stepped inside. A force seemed to cling to her as she passed through the doorway, but it didn't stop her.

Once inside, the force released her, and she looked around. There were more than a dozen people inside. None of them moved. They all looked up at the ceiling. Indistinct voices—more like breath than words—came from every direction, but no one had opened their mouths.

Beth looked back out into the room. No one was there.

"Hunter . . . Hunter?"

No answer.

She heard a creaking sound . . . and the doors began to swing shut.

She whirled around, but it was too late. The doors slammed shut behind her.

She was locked inside the Cabinet of Souls.

CHAPTER 18

BETH HAD TO DO SOMETHING FAST. She needed to get out!

When she looked back at the people around her, they hadn't moved. She needed to get some answers . . .

The closest person was a teenage boy. Then she looked down the row. All the people were teenagers close to her own age. They didn't move. They all looked up at the ceiling, but they didn't move.

Then Beth realized most of them were wearing clothing from the past. Some wore clothes from the 1950s. Others were dressed in old-fashioned trousers and dresses that looked like they came from the nineteenth century.

Maybe they're costumes, Beth told herself. A chill went up her back. What if they *weren't* costumes? *What if these people have been here for years and years?*

Beth couldn't make any sense of it. It was fascinating and terrifying. But she was in the Hall of Horrors, after all. Maybe it was all just fake.

But somehow she knew it wasn't a trick. There was something truly horrible in this place.

She listened to the whimpers and moans the teenagers were making. Still they did not look at her. They just looked up. She wondered if they even knew she was there.

"Souls," she whispered. That must be what these people were.

Raising her voice, she spoke to the young man in front of her. "Who are you?"

No response.

"Can you hear me?"

No response.

Beth walked along the row of teenagers. A Native American girl, a girl in a flapper dress from the 1920s, a young man in an out-of-date suit. She paused when she noticed something hanging from his side. Squatting, she saw it was a pocket watch. The time was exactly twelve o'clock. And she guessed it wasn't twelve noon. She was sure the watch had stopped at midnight.

The moans continued. Beth went to the next row. There was a teenage boy dressed in a 1930s sweater and trousers. He looked ready to take a drive in his roadster. His wristwatch was visible. The hands were also frozen at twelve.

Something had happened at midnight to stop these teenagers' watches. What?

She hurried back toward the door, and then stopped abruptly. She knew that girl! The blonde curly hair and the hoodie with FEDERSON HIGH SCHOOL printed across the front. It was Andrea Payton, the girl who'd disappeared.

"Are you Andrea?" Beth asked.

No reply . . . just moans.

The cabinet doors opened with a loud creak. Beth wanted to get out of there fast, but she froze when she saw who was entering.

Ghouls and vampires and a witch and goblins of all sizes and shapes staggered through the cabinet doors. She could hear their groans as they drew closer. She was about to scream, but the frightening creatures did not approach her. One line of creatures went to her right, and the second line moved to the left. It was as if they didn't see her.

As she stared at the scary creatures, they merged with the teenagers from the cabinet. Beth was stunned. Right before her eyes, the creatures disappeared . . . sinking into the bodies of the teenagers! The teens sagged slightly and shut their eyes.

A moment later, the monsters were gone.

And the moaning ended.

Beth tried to make sense of what she'd seen. It was hard to believe that the monsters were kids her age . . .

How was that even possible?

The doors of the cabinet began to close. Beth ran toward them, determined to get out.

Inexorably, the light between the two doors grew smaller and smaller. In just a moment, they'd close, leaving her stuck inside.

"No! No! No!" Beth cried.

There was no way she could make it out in time.

Beth was doomed to become a monster in the Cabinet of Souls.

CHAPTER 19

BETH THREW HERSELF TOWARD THE
doors, twisting her body and squeezing through at the last possible second.

Safely outside, she collapsed on the floor.

She was amazed to see Hunter standing right where she'd left him. He helped her to her feet. "There you are! I lost you. Where did you go?"

"I was inside of that!" She pointed at the cabinet. "We have to get out of here. Now!"

"Right," they said together, turning to the door.

Dr. Hysteria was standing there. Right between them and the door.

"Can I help you?" His skin looked even grayer than the last time she'd seen him. "Do we have a problem?"

She stared at him, not knowing what to say. Hunter was just as silent.

"You look frightened," Dr. Hysteria continued. "But then this *is* the Hall of Horrors, so I suppose that's quite the point." He looked past her. "You saw the Cabinet of Souls?"

She nodded, unable to look away from his dark eyes.

"That's a pity. It's not ready for viewing. It is to be one of our best attractions." A creepy smile curled beneath his black mustache. "But there are still some *technical* problems."

Hunter looked relieved as he bent toward Beth. "See? I told you."

But Beth didn't believe a word Dr. Hysteria had said. No one was going to fool her this time! She knew what she'd seen, but she wasn't going to argue with Dr. Hysteria. All she wanted was to get away from the Hall of Horrors. Maybe then she could figure out what had happened inside the Cabinet of Souls.

"Did you see it, too, young man?" asked Dr. Hysteria.

"No . . . sir." He added the last word as he stared at the showman. "It's a cool prop, by the way." He swallowed roughly. "Theme-park quality."

"I'm sorry I sounded harsh, but this area is for employees only," Dr. Hysteria said in a voice as sweet as sugar.

"Yeah," said Hunter. "We totally get it." He put his hand on Beth's back to steer her past Dr. Hysteria. "We'll go now."

Beth looked back at Dr. Hysteria as they stepped out into the hall. His expression was one of pure evil.

As Hunter drove back to her house, Beth told him what she'd seen in the Cabinet of Souls. He didn't say much, just stared out the windshield.

When he stopped his car in front of Beth's house, she stared out the windshield, too. She was too shaken to get out. She glanced at Hunter, who slowly looked at her.

"You don't believe me," she said.

"I believe that you believe. Okay, it's just . . . that place is all about illusion. The stuff they can do these days. Smoke and mirrors." He pointed to his head. "The mind plays tricks and all that . . ."

"Maybe, but that missing girl from Federson . . . I saw her." She couldn't get that out of her mind. Of all that had happened, seeing Andrea was the most real. She looked at Hunter. "Andrea Payton. I know I saw her."

"Are you really that sure?"

Beth saw him clamp his lips closed, as if he were afraid of saying anything more. If he said any more, he'd probably admit he thought she was crazy.

She sighed. Was it possible she'd imagined it? The inside of the cabinet was filled with mist. It had swirled around everything and everyone.

Hunter leaned toward her. "Beth, I admire you for caring so much."

She opened the door, wondering why he didn't believe her. Now she was questioning herself. Could she have been wrong about what she'd seen? If she hadn't seen Andrea, then who *had* she seen?

Beth climbed out and closed the door behind her. Then she leaned on the open window. "Thank you for coming with me tonight."

He gave a small nod and a smaller smile. "Good night."

That night, Beth couldn't sleep, so she got up and went over to her computer. She had to find out more about the Hall of Horrors.

But that wasn't enough. She needed to talk to someone. Not Hunter. She could see that he thought she'd lost her mind. She needed to talk to someone who knew her before all this crazy stuff happened.

There was only one person.

Five minutes later, she was walking across the street and knocking on Kellen's door.

He opened it, and relief surged through her. Kellen knew her. He might not believe her, but he'd known her long enough to listen.

"Hey," she said, trying to sound casual. "Can I talk to you?"

"Sure." He stepped back. "Come in."

She followed him to the living room. She smelled the wonderful scent of a fire in the fireplace. She'd spent almost as much time at his house as she had in her own. It felt good to be there. Safe.

Not sure where to start, she decided to jump right in. "I saw something tonight."

"I know. The Cabinet of Souls?"

She stared at him, shocked. "How did you know that?"

"Lilith. Dr. Hysteria told her about it."

She looked across the room to the couch under the big windows. Lilith was sitting there, looking as if she'd always been welcome at Kellen's house. She gave one of those snooty waves. The ones where each finger moves separately, like a waterfall.

Lilith stood and sashayed across the room. "Dr. Hysteria has been working on that trick for years."

"Was it cool?" asked Kellen.

"Was it cool?" Beth repeated, annoyed at both of them. She had seen something so horrible she could hardly believe it, and Kellen wanted to know if it was *cool*? "Oh, oh . . ."

Beth stopped herself. She didn't want to have this conversation in front of Lilith. She didn't trust the girl

who worked at the Hall of Horrors. And she didn't like the way Lilith had oozed her way into Kellen's company.

Beth turned to Kellen. "Why is she here?" she asked, not caring how it sounded.

"She stopped by," Kellen said. "I told you, she's cool. What did Hunter think?"

Beth waved her hands in frustration. "He thinks it's all smoke and mirrors. That's because he didn't see what I saw! He wasn't in the cabinet with me."

Lilith gave her a long stare. She held up a large gold coin. "Do you see this coin, Beth?"

"Yes."

"That's funny, because I see—" She ran her other hand up in front of the coin. In its wake, a dove was sitting on her fingers. "—a bird!"

Kellen grinned. "That's awesome."

Beth wasn't ready to give up so easily. She took out her phone and showed Lilith the screen. "What do you see here?"

It was a line drawing of a showman who looked a lot like Dr. Hysteria standing outside the Hall of Horrors. Over his head arched the words CARNIVAL OF CREEPS. She made sure Kellen got a good look.

"I found this on the web," she said. "It's from 1832."

"I know," Lilith said, and Beth deflated. "That's the inspiration for the Hall of Horrors. Dr. Hysteria copied that character's looks. But he thought 'Hall of Horrors' sounded more modern then 'Carnival of Creeps,' so he changed it."

"Oh," said Kellen, "that makes sense. So he's not almost two hundred years old."

Lilith chuckled as she stroked the dove. "Between you and me, sometimes he smells like it."

This hadn't gone at all as Beth had hoped.

Stepping toward her, Lilith held out the bird. Except now it was an orange. "Have something sweet." She gave Beth a glance, daring her to take the orange.

Beth took it. Lilith smiled and reached out to run her fingers along Kellen's jaw. She gazed directly into his eyes as she purred, "Good night."

She shot Beth a half smile. Its message was clear: if Beth wanted Kellen, she'd already lost him.

Lilith headed toward the door, pausing to give Kellen a little wave. "Bye, Kellen."

After the door closed, Kellen turned back to Beth. "Is she awesome or what? She told me she's been training the show's horses since she was a little girl."

Beth stared at him. She didn't think Lilith was awesome at all. "Kellen, I'm scared for you. If she knows about the Cabinet of Souls, then she's obviously in on it."

"In on what? What are you talking about?" His voice grew sharp. "Y'know what? You can start going out with Hunter, but as soon as a girl pays any attention to me, she's part of some evil plot."

"This isn't about that! Besides, I'm not 'going out' with Hunter."

He gave her a look that told her he didn't believe her.

"Okay," she hurried to say. "This thing was scary. I'm not positive, but I think I saw that missing girl in there. From Federson. Andrea Payton."

"You're really trippin', Beth."

Beth was shocked. This wasn't the Kellen she'd known forever. He wasn't the same Kellen she'd known just a couple of days ago. He was changed. Different.

There could be only one explanation.

"Kellen . . . that girl, Lilith. Don't trust her. I mean it. I'm worried about you."

"You think this new person comes to town, and all of a sudden, I start acting crazy. That's not true." His eyes drilled into her. "That's not me."

She wanted to say it wasn't her, either, but she could tell he wouldn't listen.

"Wow," she said softly. "Hey, I know a disappearing act, too."

She handed him the orange and left, feeling more alone than ever.

Beth didn't fall asleep for hours. When she finally did, she heard a voice calling her. "Beth . . . Beth . . ."

She sat up in bed and gasped. Even in the dark, she could see the person whose voice she'd heard in her dreams. Dr. Hysteria.

Beth gasped. Dr. Hysteria was in her room. He was standing at the foot of her bed. How had he gotten into her house? Why was he here? He looked even scarier in the dark, dark room.

"You've met Andrea," he said in icy voice. "Andrea, tell Beth what you told me."

A girl's voice came out of the darkness. She was crouched on the floor. "You can't save me."

"Tell her to her face," Dr. Hysteria ordered.

Andrea threw off her hoodie. Her face wasn't hers. It belonged to a gremlin. "Please save me!" she begged Beth.

Beth bolted up out of her pillows, panting as if she'd run a marathon. She scanned the room.

There was no one there.

It must have been a dream. It had to be a dream.

But what if it wasn't?

CHAPTER 20

THE HALL OF HORRORS did NOT LOOK

frightening in the morning light. It looked old and drab—
as if all its magic couldn't stand up to the sunshine.

Deep inside, Dr. Hysteria looked weak, too. As he
threw open the doors to the Cabinet of Souls, he was
gasping for each breath.

"Must feed," he said, leaning heavily on the doors.
Even his voice had lost its strength.

Taking a couple of shallow breaths, he pulled himself
through the doorway. He struggled to part the mist clinging to the floor. On both sides, the trapped souls stood,
staring and moaning.

Fear was more alive than anything else in the cabinet.
There was the fear from the trapped souls who had seen
what their end would be. And there was the fear from Dr.
Hysteria. He was afraid that he would run out of the
young souls that kept him alive.

He moved toward a girl who wore a 1950s-style dress. He leaned closer and breathed in deeply.

A wave of her life force came out of her body—her soul. It lingered a moment in the air before Dr. Hysteria drew it into himself.

His steps were stronger as he moved to his next victim. Draining too much too fast from a trapped soul would ruin his chances of getting every drop of the essence he needed.

Next in line was Andrea Payton. As he leaned forward and drew in a deep breath, her body arched. She fought to hold on to what was hers and hers alone. But Dr. Hysteria was too powerful, and soon her soul flowed out of her. She moaned as her body sagged. Once again he had stolen life from her.

Dr. Hysteria moved on to his next victim. This girl was dressed in pioneer clothing.

Dr. Hysteria paused. "You're almost empty," he said. Then he breathed in the last of the girl's life force. What remained crumbled into nothingness. The girl became part of the mist floating above the floor. Soon even that had disappeared, and all that was left was her old linen dress.

"You were a good worker," Dr. Hysteria said. "But tonight, we get fresh souls. Chop-chop! Let's get to work."

All around him, his creatures emerged from their trapped souls. Soon the room was filled with ghouls and ghosts and monsters. They formed two lines and paraded out of the Cabinet of Souls.

Dr. Hysteria laughed his most wicked laugh. The lives he had stolen had made him strong again. He was ready to capture new ones.

And tonight was Halloween! How perfect. By midnight, many fresh souls would take their place in the Cabinet of Souls.

Yes, and he had his eye on several of the visitors to the Hall of Horrors. They were almost ready for his dining pleasure . . .

CHAPTER 21

"NICOLE!" BETH CALLED AS SHE
walked into school on Halloween morning.

Her friend didn't turn around.

Beth knew it had to be Nicole. Although her friend never went anywhere with her hair looking so ratty and tangled. On the other hand, it had to be Nicole, because no one else in school had such fabulous shoes.

So why didn't she stop? Maybe she hadn't heard Beth calling her.

She tried again, running to catch up with her friend. "Hey, Nicole!"

Nicole spun around, and Beth stared. Her friend looked . . . possessed! There wasn't any other word for it. Her makeup was dark and scary—a little bit like Lilith's—and her face was so pale she looked gray. Was she sick?

It couldn't be a Halloween costume. Nicole loved dressing up, but she always wore glamorous costumes. She would never make herself look like some fright queen.

"What?" demanded her friend in a voice Beth had never heard. She sounded like someone who was filled with hate. Beth knew Nicole could be self-centered, and a bit obsessed with boys, but she'd never been hateful.

Until now.

"Have you been getting my texts?" Beth's question was cautious as she stared at a Nicole she didn't recognize.

Nicole sneered. "Yeah, about five hundred of them. It's annoying. I turned off my phone." She took on a whiny voice. "Queen Beth says there's an emergency, and everyone's supposed to jump." Her face turned fierce. "Get real."

Beth looked away, unable to meet her friend's angry gaze. Her eyes fell on Nicole's hand. Nicole was scratching the spot where Dr. Hysteria's stamp was still visible. Her skin was raw and red and infected.

"What's going on with your hand?" she asked.

Nicole just grunted and stalked away.

"Nicole!" Beth called. She started to follow her friend, and then stopped. Nicole obviously didn't want to talk to her. What was wrong with her?

Outside the school, Kellen was scuffing his shoes along the sidewalk. He was alone. He didn't know where Luke was. Usually his friend trailed along with him, cracking

jokes the whole way. Kellen hadn't realized how much he missed having him around. He'd catch up with Luke later. Maybe he would ask him to tell one of his stupid jokes.

"Good morning," purred a voice he couldn't forget.

Lilith was standing right behind him. She looked good in her black leather jacket and pants. He glanced past her, but he didn't see her motorcycle.

"Oh . . . hi," he said.

"I spoke to Dr. Hysteria about you. Told him that I knew a guy who might be great in the show."

"Me?" He was flattered. After the dance contest, he wasn't so scared about making a fool of himself in public. The actors in the Hall of Horrors seemed to get into their parts big-time. It could be fun.

"Are you interested? You'd get to be a character in our Halloween finale."

"Really? Cool."

"Then let's go." She turned to walk back in the direction she'd come. Away from school.

"Now? I have school."

"And school will be here tomorrow, but I won't." She gave him a sweet smile.

The bell rang.

"That's the warning bell," he said. "I'm going to be late for class."

"And if you don't follow your heart, you're going to be

late for life." She put her arm around his shoulders and steered him away from school.

He stared at her. He'd always been the good kid. The one who followed the rules. What had it gotten him? Bad Boy Hunter came to town, and Beth fell head over heels for him.

This was his chance to do something Good Boy Kellen would never do.

"Let's go," he said.

She smiled and led him away. He followed her readily, without looking back once.

Beth was worried. She couldn't find Nicole. Where could she have gone? The hallway was crowded because home-room didn't start for another five minutes. As she passed other kids, hanging out by their lockers and making plans for Halloween, she glanced at their hands. None of them had Dr. Hysteria's stamp. But she recognized several of the kids who'd been in their group when they went through the Hall of Horrors that first time.

She stopped by a locker where Dan and Theresa, whom she knew from English class, were chatting.

"Hi," she said, feeling awkward about what she wanted to ask. "Have you guys been to Dr. Hysteria's Hall of Horrors yet?"

Dan grinned. "Yeah, it was awesome."

"Not that scary." Theresa rolled her eyes.

"Some of it was funny," he said. "Those zombies were great!"

Beth kept her smile in place. "By any chance, did they stamp your hand?"

"Yeah, they did," Dan said. "But it just washed off."

Theresa looked down at her hand. "I can still kinda see mine."

"Not anymore." He licked his finger and grabbed her hand. Tilting it, he rubbed off the last of Dr. Hysteria's image.

"Ew! Gross!" Theresa complained. She snatched her hand away and gave him a dirty look.

Beth turned away and started walking. That stamp had come off of Theresa's hand so easily. Beth had scrubbed hers, and it still was as bright as the night it had been stamped.

She stopped and glanced around. Nobody was paying attention to her. Licking her thumb, she tried to rub off the stamp the way Dan had.

Nothing happened.

Nasty laughter floated from farther along the hall. Forgetting the stamp, Beth looked up and saw Luke taunting a boy whose curly hair stuck up in every direction.

"That hairdo is a *hair-don't*," Luke said, loud enough for all the boys gathered around him to hear.

Why was he hanging out with those creeps? He liked to make jokes, but it wasn't like Luke to be mean.

First Nicole was acting strange, now Luke. What was going on?

"Did you stick your finger in a light socket, Brillo pad?" Luke crowed. "Puffball? Poodle head?"

The curly-haired kid cringed at the laughter. Shutting his locker, he turned to walk away.

That didn't stop Luke. "Hey, nice perm! 1980 called. They want their hairdo back."

That brought more laughs from the bullies. Luke fist-bumped the four guys in his audience.

Beth pushed past one of them and looked Luke directly in the eye. "Dude, that was really mean!"

"Yeah, so who cares?" Luke fired back as he scratched a bandage over his left hand. "I was getting laughs."

"What happened to your hand?" she asked. She could see a hint of the Dr. Hysteria stamp beneath the bandage. Was Luke's hand as raw as Nicole's had been? If he kept scratching it, his skin would be bright red, too.

"What happened to your face? Score! Hoo-hoo!" He bounced away and around a corner.

"What?" Beth wondered if all her friends had gone crazy. She hadn't seen Kellen, but he'd acted weird last night when she'd gone over to his house. She thought it was just because Lilith was there. But this was too strange.

What was happening to her friends?

Luke bounded into the boys' restroom, still laughing. His jokes had rocked this morning. His new posse had laughed at every one. The meaner he got, the more they laughed.

Dr. Hysteria was right. He didn't need his old friends. They didn't get him and his sense of humor.

He ran in circles like an ape, letting his arms hang down and making silly sounds. He made faces at himself in the mirror. He was *so* funny! Everything was perfect.

Except for that itch on his hand. The stupid bandage was in the way. He tore it off and tossed it aside. He scratched the red, scaly skin on his hand around the stamp. It itched. It itched so bad.

Then he heard a voice. It seemed to be coming from his hand. It was the voice of Dr. Hysteria. And his words gave Luke a chill.

"Now you're mine," Dr. Hysteria said.

Luke looked up to see where the showman was. But he forgot all about Dr. Hysteria when he looked in the mirror.

What he saw there was the scariest thing he had ever seen.

CHAPTER 22

LUKE STARED AT HIS REFLECTION.

He could hardly believe it was him. He was wearing a bright, fuzzy wig. His face was painted white. He had large lips colored with bright red lipstick. There were blue circles around his eyes. And on his nose was a red ball.

He was a clown! A real clown!

And not just a regular clown. He also had sharp fangs. He was an evil, fiendish clown!

He took one more look and let out a loud, evil whoop.

"Oh, yeah!" he shouted with joy.

His laugh echoed through the bathroom. As he dashed out into the now-empty hall, he did flips and kicked up his heels and laughed and laughed and laughed.

Kellen led Lilith along the back way students used when they wanted to cut class. They went through a few backyards and came out on a street several blocks over.

The clip-clop of horse's hooves sounded behind them. Kellen glanced at Lilith. How had she known to have her horse and buggy waiting here?

They stepped into the street, and the horse stopped right in front of them. Kellen got the oddest feeling that the horse was looking directly at him, as if it were trying to tell him something. He knew it was just his imagination, but he couldn't get the idea out of his mind.

"Want to drive?" Lilith asked.

"Yeah," he said. Being the guy with the reins made him feel like a real man. And sitting next to such a beautiful girl felt pretty cool, too.

As they began climbing up into the buggy, Lilith stroked the horse's jaw. "Hello, handsome," she murmured.

The horse whinnied as Kellen swung up into the buggy and grasped the reins.

Lilith slid closer to him and put her hand on his arm. He flexed his muscle, just so she could feel it. She smiled up at him.

This was going to be fun.

Beth headed for her next class. Everything felt off today . . . and not just because it was Halloween. Nice guy Luke was acting like a bully and her best friend wouldn't even talk to her.

She spotted Nicole sitting in their usual spot. She was painting her fingernails black. Beth had never seen her wear that color. She looked at Nicole and realized that she was dressed completely in black. The only color on her was the red rings under her eyes.

Beth put her books on her desk and sat down. When she looked at Nicole, her friend fixed her with a glare so cold it could have frozen a pool of lava. Beth tried to think of something to say, but couldn't.

Their teacher, Ms. Sarkosian, came into the room. She loved Halloween and was dressed in elf ears in honor of the day. She clapped her hands as she circled toward the front of the room.

"Hello, everyone," she said cheerfully. "Has everyone made their Halloween plans?" She touched her fake ears. "Today we're going to work on our history packets. So please get them out and work quietly at your desks."

Papers rustled around the room as the students took out their work.

"Has anyone seen Luke?" Ms. Sarkosian asked. "Is he in school?"

"I saw him when I was in the hallway earlier," Beth answered.

"How about Kellen?"

Beth looked at the desk on her other side. Where *was* Kellen? He hadn't looked sick last night. And he never skipped school.

Ms. Sarkosian frowned and made a mark on her seating chart before picking up some papers from her desk.

Beth glanced at Nicole. Her friend looked as if she was in a haze.

Suddenly Nicole leaned forward and *hissed*! A forked tongue shot out of her mouth!

Beth couldn't believe her eyes. Was Nicole really there at the next desk?

Nobody else had noticed. They all were doing their history packets.

Nicole stood up. When she spoke, her voice was raspy, "Ms. Sarkosian, may I use the hall pass?"

The teacher raised her eyes briefly, and then replied, "Go ahead."

Again Beth looked around the room, but everyone was focused on their work. Was she the only one who heard the ominous hiss in Nicole's words?

Nicole smirked as she walked to Ms. Sarkosian's desk and picked up the hall pass, a round piece of cardboard

with a key attached. She strode past Beth toward the door. Before she went out, she sneered at Beth.

"Ms. Sarkosian," asked Beth, fearing what might happen to her friend if she was left alone, "May I go, too?"

"No," the teacher replied. "One at a time."

Beth stared at the door. Nicole wasn't herself. Something was terribly wrong with her. She shouldn't be by herself, but Beth couldn't go after her. Even if she tried to explain to Ms. Sarkosian, would the teacher believe her? Ms. Sarkosian hadn't seemed to notice anything different about Nicole.

Someone had to do something. Beth didn't know what she was going to do—but one thing was clear: Her friends were in danger. And it was up to her to help them.

CHAPTER 23

DURING THE DAY, THE TOWN SQUARE
was quiet. Even the wind was barely blowing, though it
sent a few pieces of paper twisting between the harvest
festival's booths.

Crazy laughter shattered the silence. Grinning fiercely
in his new clown face, Luke sprinted into the middle of
the street and began doing cartwheels. He kicked up his
feet. He laughed. He did flips. Everything was funny, and
it was all thanks to him. He wanted to shout for everyone
to laugh, but there was nobody to listen.

Luke did a flip over a bale of hay. When he landed
back on his feet, he saw Dr. Hysteria in front of him. He
had reached the Hall of Horrors.

"Ho-ho. Hee-hee. Ha-ha!" Luke shouted. He suddenly realized he couldn't say anything else. But it was
okay. He was a clown. He could make everyone laugh
with just those few words.

A tall, bald ghoul in a karate gi and a short goblin stood next to the entrance to the Hall of Horrors.

Dr. Hysteria pointed to Luke and said in a bored tone, "Get him into costume."

The ghoul and the goblin stepped forward.

"Yes, yes, a costume," Luke the clown crowed. "Ha-ha-ha-ha!" Words had come back to him. He wanted a costume. That would make his jokes even funnier. Everyone loves a clown, don't they? Everyone would love him and his jokes. Nobody would tell him to stop clowning around ever again.

"Tailored just for you." Dr. Hysteria handed the goblin a set of clothes and huge clown shoes.

The ghoul and the goblin grabbed Luke's arms and herded him into the Hall of Horrors. Luke laughed at the huge picture of Dr. Hysteria. "That's a big nose!" he shouted.

The goblin just growled.

"Good lad," Dr. Hysteria said. He surveyed the street with an expectant smile. The first one was here. The others wouldn't be far behind. By midnight, he would be able to feast.

Beth couldn't stand waiting any longer. She walked up to Ms. Sarkosian's desk.

"Yes?" asked the teacher.

"Nicole's been gone a really long time now," Beth said. "Do you think I could go and check on her?"

"Go ahead." Ms. Sarkosian wrote out another hall pass and handed it to her. She gave Beth a look that warned her there better not be any mischief afoot.

Beth hurried out into the empty hall. Nicole had turned left out of the room, so she went that way. After a few more steps, *something* rushed at her.

Beth stared in shock. It was a witch. Her hands were claws, her face wrinkled and warty and hideous.

The witch ran full-speed into Beth, knocking her to the floor like a linebacker tackling a running back. All the air burst out of Beth in a gasp.

The witch gripped the front of Beth's shirt and shrieked in her face. Her breath smelled worse than road-kill. Her beady eyes bored into Beth's.

The next moment, the witch jumped to her feet and jerked Beth up with inhuman strength. Again she roared in Beth's face, showing her rotten teeth.

Beth looked down. The witch was wearing familiar clothes. They were Nicole's.

"Nicole?" she asked, not wanting to believe what she was seeing.

The witch hurled her away, and Beth slammed into a row of lockers and slid to the floor.

For a moment, she just lay there, trying to breathe—

and trying to accept what she'd seen and heard. She struggled to get up. Every inch of her body ached from Nicole's blow.

She pushed herself up to her elbows. The hall was deserted. Nicole was gone.

Beth had a bad feeling about where Nicole had gone. Her stomach ached at the thought of what had happened to her best friend.

It was so clear now . . . and so awful. All the people trapped in the Cabinet of Souls were teenagers once. They had all vanished.

Now her friends were next. And Dr. Hysteria was behind it all.

She had to stop him. But she couldn't do this by herself. She needed help.

But who was left to help her? All her friends were gone.

Beth was alone.

CHAPTER

24

BETH SAT IN THE PRINCIPAL'S OFFICE.

On the other side of the desk, Principal Callahan watched her. Behind him stood Ms. Sarkosian and Sheriff Wilson. She'd told them everything she'd seen and heard.

They looked at her as if she'd lost her mind.

How could she convince them?

"It's Dr. Hysteria," she insisted. She had to get them to listen to her. She knew that what she had to say sounded crazy. But it was crazy true. "He's turning teenagers into monsters, and he's taking their souls. He collects them in this cabinet—the Cabinet of Souls—which according to my research probably makes him some kind of minor demon. He's keeping them for later so he can feed off of them. And now he has my friends—Kellen, Luke, Nicole. They're all missing. I think he's going to take their souls, too, if I don't stop him by midnight. Tonight!"

Ms. Sarkosian and the sheriff exchanged a worried look while the principal stared at her over his coffee cup.

"Right," said the sheriff, crossing his arms and giving Beth a smile that hinted it'd be best if she were sedated before she hurt herself or others.

"This is my most steady student," Ms. Sarkosian said with a sympathetic smile.

Beth smiled back, encouraging her teacher. She doubted Ms. Sarkosian believed her, but she was willing to give her the benefit of the doubt.

"Straight As," Ms. Sarkosian went on. "The good citizenship award. And there are kids missing."

The principal just stared, but the sheriff sighed.

Beth hoped that meant he was going to help. She didn't know where else to turn.

Half an hour later, the sheriff's patrol car rolled up in front of the Hall of Horrors. Beth sat in the passenger's seat.

"He's really, really dangerous," Beth warned the sheriff as he unlatched his seat belt.

Sheriff Wilson looked down at his service revolver.

"A gun isn't going to do you any good against a demon," she said.

"Okay, then," he said, and she knew he was just humoring her. "How am I supposed to stop a, er, demon?"

"I don't know."

"Right." He grumbled. "Then you stay here and figure that out while I go have a look around." He got out. As he closed the door, he gave her a warning look. Its message was clear: She better not set as much as a toenail outside the car.

As the sheriff approached the Hall of Horrors, Dr. Hysteria stepped out.

"Hello, Sheriff Wilson," Dr. Hysteria said, as if he'd been expecting company. "How may I be of service?"

Beth shuddered. Was his polite smile just another way Dr. Hysteria twisted people to his will?

Sheriff Wilson looked embarrassed. "The girl says that you're a de—" He couldn't say the words. "She says that there may be some missing kids here."

"Really?" drawled Dr. Hysteria, still smiling. His eyes, cold as a snake's, shifted toward Beth, and she shivered again. "She said that?"

"So I was wondering," the sheriff said, "if I could have a look around?"

"By all means."

"Thank you."

Listening to the sheriff, Beth wasn't sure if he was thanking Dr. Hysteria for letting him look around or for not laughing in his face at the peculiar request.

Dr. Hysteria's smile turned into a scowl as the sheriff walked past him. His eyes blazed with fury as he focused on Beth.

She was starting to think letting him know she suspected him had been a big mistake.

Then he smiled at her. It was the smile of someone who knew he was going to win. He turned and followed the sheriff into the Hall of Horrors.

Beth hugged her knees to her chest. How was she going to protect her friends . . . *and* herself?

Inside, Dr. Hysteria led Sheriff Wilson into the zombie classroom. The light was dim, but not frightening.

"Did you want to look at my permits?" Dr. Hysteria asked. "The originals are all filed at city hall."

"No, no. That's okay." The sheriff was getting the creeps. He just wanted to find out if there was any truth to Beth's suspicions, and then get out of there.

Dr. Hysteria went over to a switch on the wall. "Showbiz magic. It's amazing what it can do to the imagination." He flipped it up.

Lights flashed. Ghostly laughter and screams came from all around them. Doors creaked, and moans echoed as if from the depths of the earth. A painting dropped to the floor, and a fake skeleton with glowing eyes jumped forward, growling. A trapdoor popped up from the teacher's desk, and the head of a hairy beast sprang up from underneath it.

Sheriff Wilson flinched. He couldn't help it. The place was spooky.

Dr. Hysteria flipped the switch back up. Instantly, the lights returned to normal, and it was quiet again. The picture slid back into place, hiding the skeleton again. The trapdoor closed on the desk.

"Wow," Sheriff Wilson said with an ironic smile. "I get your point."

"Indeed." Dr. Hysteria motioned back in the direction from which they'd come. "After you."

Satisfied, the sheriff walked out of the room. He didn't glance over his shoulder, or he would have seen the grim expression on Dr. Hysteria's face.

The demon didn't like anyone interfering with his plans. He was going to make Beth pay for the trouble she'd caused him.

Soon.

Beth was doing research on her phone when a movement in the rearview mirror caught her eye. Kellen and Lilith were walking past the sheriff's car.

"Kellen!" She opened the car door and jumped out.

Kellen didn't stop. He just kept walking with Lilith. It reminded her too much of the way Nicole was acting.

"Kellen!" She ran to his side and grabbed his arm.

Just then, the sheriff and Dr. Hysteria emerged from the Hall of Horrors.

Sheriff Wilson headed over to Beth. "Is this one of the missing boys?" he asked her.

"This is Kellen," she said.

"Missing?" Kellen asked, looking at the sheriff in confusion. "I'm not missing. I'm right here." He frowned at her. "You said I was missing?"

Beth tried to salvage the situation. "Well, he's not himself. And he wasn't at school . . ." She knew that she sounded weak. But she also knew that her friends were in terrible danger—even if they didn't believe it.

Kellen gave the sheriff a look that said he didn't have any idea what she was talking about.

Dr. Hysteria stared at Beth expressionlessly. That was scarier than one of his scowls.

Beth knew that this was her only chance. She couldn't waste it.

"I'll show you." She ran past the others and into the Hall of Horrors.

"Wait!" called the sheriff. "No—" There was a note of genuine fear in his voice. He really didn't want to go back into that freaky place.

"Oh, my!" said Dr. Hysteria, turning to follow Beth.

Kellen, Lilith, and the sheriff went with him. As they walked through the corridors, it was oddly silent.

"I really don't like her running around back here," Dr. Hysteria said, sounding very sincere. "She could get hurt."

They came to an intersection, and everyone looked both ways. Beth was nowhere in sight.

"Boy, this is quite a maze you've got here." The sheriff was careful about where he stepped.

"It's all modular. We move it around during the show." He gave a short laugh. "Sometimes even I get lost."

Ahead of them, Beth retraced the steps she and Hunter had taken the night they'd discovered the Cabinet of Souls. Could it have been only last night? It seemed a lifetime ago. And if she wanted to save Andrea Payton and her friends and the other trapped souls, she needed to prove that Dr. Hysteria was truly a demon.

There! That was the door she'd gone through when she saw the vampire and the zombie. She opened it and, to her relief, recognized the next corridor as well. She kept running.

After a few more turns, she'd discovered the door she'd gone through last night. It was slightly ajar, so she crept inside.

The Cabinet of Souls stood across from her. It was silent as a tomb. Not a single moan came from it.

No matter, Beth told herself. She'd found it, and now she could show the sheriff what was inside.

"I found it!" she called.

A moment later, Dr. Hysteria appeared. The wide-eyed sheriff, Kellen, and Lilith were right behind him. They all stared at her.

She pointed toward the cabinet. "This is what I was talking about. Andrea Payton is in here."

"This is an expensive prop," Dr. Hysteria said, "and it's not ready. Don't go near it!"

"Right," Beth said with a tight laugh. He wasn't going to stop her that easily. She knew what she had seen. Nobody was going to talk her out of it. Not again. She grabbed the handles on the doors.

"Please, don't!" Dr. Hysteria cried.

Beth ignored him. She yanked on the doors, and they creaked open.

Inside, there was nothing but a sheet of black plywood. The fake front wobbled, and then crashed down, leaving Beth standing in what had been the doorway. Pieces of broken plywood were scattered around her.

The Cabinet of Souls was gone.

Whirling, she saw a snide smile on Lilith's lips. Worse, Kellen was looking at *her* with pity.

Now everyone thought she'd lost her mind.

Beth was beginning to think they were right.

CHAPTER 25

HOW HAD THEY DONE IT?

As Beth sat in the sheriff's car, she couldn't think of an answer. She was frustrated, and she had no idea what to do next.

But she knew what she'd seen. She knew she wasn't crazy. The satisfied smiles on both Dr. Hysteria and Lilith's faces made her angry, but they also made her determined to find the real Cabinet of Souls. Dr. Hysteria and Lilith were evil. They had to be stopped. And she would do it.

But how?

She watched Dr. Hysteria emerge from the Hall of Horrors with Sheriff Wilson.

"There's no reason to make a legal case out of it," said Dr. Hysteria. "I believe the young lady just got wrapped up in the spirit of the season."

Sheriff Wilson couldn't hide his relief that the whole situation was over. All he wanted was to get far away from the Hall of Horrors. "That's very decent of you. I'll get her back to her parents now."

Beth sighed. She wouldn't get any more help from the sheriff. Not that he had been much help anyhow. He hadn't believed her from the start. He'd been easily charmed by Dr. Hysteria's smooth talk. She had to figure out what she was going to do next to save her friends.

Kellen and Lilith were standing by the VIP entrance, listening to the two men talk. Kellen pulled out his phone and punched in a number.

"I'm calling Beth," he said when Lilith looked at him with a faint frown. It should have been obvious. He was puzzled by Beth's weird behavior, but she was still one of his best friends. "I feel bad for her."

"I do, too." Lilith said. She reached out and took his phone. "But we can't fix everyone's problems. C'mon. Let me show you something."

She opened the VIP door and went in. Curious, Kellen followed her. They were walking down a corridor Kellen hadn't seen before.

"Do you know why trapeze artists are able to perform such death-defying tricks?" Lilith asked him.

"No."

"They practice with a safety net. People are more willing to take risks if they have something to fall back on."

She stopped and faced him. "So I'm curious, Kellen. Are you Beth's safety net?"

Her words cut into him. He didn't want to be anyone's safety net. He didn't want to be someone's Plan B in case Plan A didn't work out.

But he realized he'd been acting that way. And that was going to stop. Now.

"No." He shook his head.

"Then I think you're ready," Lilith said.

"Ready for what?"

She looked past him, and he turned to see a brightly lit sign. MAGIC THEATER.

"What's so magic about it?" he asked.

"It's where you will see what truly feeds your soul," she said. "Once you've seen that, you're under my spell."

He grinned. "I think I already am under your spell."

She stepped back and pulled open the curtain. "Enter."

Kellen looked around the small theater as they walked in. He followed Lilith to the center aisle between the rows of folding chairs. Mist crawled up around his legs. Lilith glanced from him to the stage, so he looked there, too.

"Now watch," she ordered.

Lightning flashed. A window seemed to open in front of him. Loud rock music—the kind played in movies when a superhero does something amazing—blasted into the theater.

The scene before him was a city street. It looked like a bomb had gone off. Fires burned in gutted vehicles. The windows of nearby buildings were dark.

One person stood straight and tall in the middle of the destruction. Kellen! He was dressed in what looked like leather armor. He gazed over the fires, searching for the one who needed him to be her hero.

"There you are," Lilith said, but her voice was distant and unearthly.

What he saw in front of him was *real*. As real as a dream come true. He was a warrior. A hero. The one who could be depended on to save the day.

"That's me!" he exclaimed.

And there was Beth, walking toward him, in an outfit made of the same black leather. Hers was decorated with lace. Not frilly lace, but netting that was somehow both powerful and beautiful. Her hair was done in a style he'd never seen her wear. Pulled back and teased up with a trio of braids draped over her ears. The rest hung wild and free down her back.

She looked straight ahead. She looked at nothing but him.

Just him.

A black car sped toward them through the piles of trash and burning cars. Hunter's car.

In the scene, he and Beth turned as one to face the

newcomer. Her face showed her fear. His own was determined and ready for battle.

Hunter got out of the car. He was dressed in black leather, too, but his suit was dusty and worn. He didn't look like a hero. His face was dirty, and his lip curled in a sneer. "Hey!" he called. "She's mine!"

Kellen smiled and shook his head. What a loser!

"You *dare* challenge me?" Hunter threw his hands out wide, inviting Kellen to throw the first punch.

Kellen stood his ground. "Bring it," he said, with a dangerous undertone of his own.

In the theater, Kellen grinned. Now *that* was the way a hero answered a bully.

Hunter ran toward him, and Kellen raced to meet him. They were like two bulls about to lock horns. Only one would be left standing. The one that would win Beth.

Kellen didn't slow down for the burning vehicle in front of him. He leaped, somersaulting over the top of it. Landing on his feet lightly, he turned to face his foe.

Hunter swung. Kellen leaned back, letting Hunter spin off balance when his fist didn't connect. Kellen struck out with both a left and a right. He hit Hunter and drove him back a step.

Then Hunter hit him in the chin. Once, twice.

Kellen reeled backward. He couldn't let Hunter win. Beth deserved better than Hunter. She deserved a real hero.

Like Kellen.

Fortified by that thought, Kellen jumped into the fray. Hunter got him with a strong kick that drove him into an old wooden door leaning against a burning car. Kellen hit it hard and dropped to the ground.

He was down, but he wasn't out. Heroes don't quit.

He rushed Hunter. He avoided his foe's punches and rammed his shoulder into Hunter's gut. As his enemy folded, Kellen leaped onto his back, wrapping his arms around Hunter's waist and shoulders. He kicked up into a flip. Hunter was dragged along with him. He slammed Hunter onto a wooden pallet. It cracked, and Hunter didn't move for a long minute.

Pushing himself to his feet, Hunter stared at Kellen. The arrogance in his eyes was gone. In its place were uncertainty and fear.

Hunter lurched away, reeling from his defeat.

Beth smiled at Kellen—her hero! She stepped forward, her expression filled with admiration. She took his hand.

Together, they walked away, leaving Hunter behind.

Kellen opened the door of Hunter's car for Beth, and she stepped into the passenger seat. He got behind the wheel, and he and Beth drove away.

Kellen had won the girl, the car, and the day!

Lightning flashed, blinding Kellen. The light flickered silver in his eyes as the scene vanished.

He blinked, unable to remember the past few minutes. Pain ground through him, and he groaned.

"What just happened?" he whispered. "Where am I?"

Lilith smiled, but it wasn't one of her mysterious smiles. It was cold and merciless . . . and hungry. "You're in my father's power now."

Her father? What was she talking about?

His hand began to itch. He looked at it. The stamp of Dr. Hysteria seemed to speak. "Mine," it intoned. "Now . . . you . . . are . . . mine!"

Lilith gave a laugh that sounded just like Dr. Hysteria's.

"*He's* your father?" Kellen asked in horror and disbelief. "No! That can't be true." He winced as sharp pain shot through him again. It came from the stamp, and spread into every inch of him. "You tricked me."

He gave a gasp of agony and clutched his wrist. Dr. Hysteria's stamp faded as his hand began to change. His fingers grew long and became claws. His nails stretched into talons. He was turning into some kind of creature. A monster!

"Beth was right!" He gasped.

"Oh, hush, dear heart," cooed Lilith. "There's nothing you can do now."

"I've got to get out of here!" He ran from the theater.

Lilith didn't bother to chase him. She just smiled.

This one had been fun.

KELLEN ESCAPED THE THEATER, BUT

stumbled along the twisting hallways outside. He couldn't go any farther. He was bent nearly in half with pain.

He was a fool! Why hadn't he listened to Beth? She'd warned him about Lilith.

Every thought disappeared as his body contorted and rearranged itself. He sank to the floor, putting his hands—no, his claws!—over his face.

Agony seared him. He threw back his head to cry out.

He roared. Like a beast.

Pulling his claws from his face, he could feel the transformation becoming complete. His nose had turned into a snout, and his teeth were fangs. He was no longer human. He was a beast. A horrible, ghoulish beast.

He dropped to his knees, weakened by the process of transformation. He couldn't even get back to his feet. Every bit of his strength had been sucked up by Lilith's evil magic. He bowed his head in surrender.

Footsteps came toward him. He saw two figures moving in the shadows at the end of the hall. They stepped into the dim light. He stared at them in disbelief.

He knew them. It was Luke and Nicole.

But they weren't the Luke and Nicole who'd first come to the Hall of Horrors with him. Luke wore the frightening makeup and costume of a fiendish clown. Pretty Nicole was a hideous hag with a black cloak that flapped over her shoulders like raven's wings.

They marched toward him in a silence that was terrifying. He should run. He should get out while he still could.

But he couldn't move. He was too exhausted.

He wasn't anyone's hero. He couldn't even save himself.

Luke and Nicole stopped on either side of Kellen.

From behind him, Kellen heard Dr. Hysteria's voice. "It does my heart good to see three good friends together."

Lilith came to stand beside her father as Luke and Nicole helped Kellen to his feet. He couldn't even stand on his own. His limbs were as limp as noodles.

"Now, get him into costume," Dr. Hysteria ordered. "We still have a show to do."

The hag and the clown dragged the beast that had been Kellen past the demon and his daughter.

Lilith looked them over. "There's still one missing."

Dr. Hysteria chuckled. "Not for long."

CHAPTER 27

WHEN THE DOORBELL RANG, BETH
was in no hurry to open it. She expected more trick-or-treaters.

But when she did, there were no princesses or superheroes screaming "trick or treat." There was only Hunter.

She practically dragged him in. Maybe he would listen to her. He was her last hope.

She told him about the fake cabinet . . . and about the sheriff. When she was finished, she could tell that he didn't believe her, either. But she gave it one more try. "Hunter, I saw Nicole. I'm telling you, she turned into a real, live . . ." She gulped, finding it hard to say the word. "I saw her turn into a real witch."

"Wow, Beth." He looked stunned. "I mean . . . are you sure Nicole wasn't wearing Halloween makeup or something?"

"I *was* sure. But now I don't even trust myself. Maybe some of this is in my imagination."

"There's only one way to find out," Hunter said. "We have to go back to the Hall of Horrors."

"But you don't believe me," she said.

"Like I said before, I'm here for you," Hunter said firmly. "Let's go."

She nodded, but the thought of going back to that terrifying place filled her with dread. She had told herself she would never go back there again.

But there was no choice. She had to help her friends, and she had to find Andrea Payton . . .

But she also had to stay alive.

The Hall of Horrors was open. A crowd milled around, waiting in a long line to get in to see the show.

Lilith stood in front of the entrance, doing her usual speech: "Do not feed the zombies. Beware of the ghouls. Do not look the witches in the eye." She tilted her head as Beth and Hunter walked by. She shot them a snooty smile. "Do not feed the zombies. Beware of the ghouls. Do not look the witches in the eye."

As they walked closer, the chained zombie lunged at

Beth. She pulled back, but didn't laugh as she had before. Nothing was funny about the Hall of Horrors now.

"You okay?" Hunter said, putting his arm around her shoulder.

She didn't answer as they got in line to begin the tour. Ahead of them, a ghoul was taking tickets and stamping hands. When a vampire jumped up from behind a gravestone, a couple of kids screamed and ran away. Beth wondered if it was the same vampire who had hunted her in the back rooms of the show.

"The first thing I have to do is find my friends," Beth said. She had to yell to be heard over the screams and the laughter.

"And if they're okay?"

"Then I guess I'll have to admit that it's all in my mind."

They joined a crowd going through the Hall of Horrors. The kids jostled one another, screamed at the characters, and laughed when someone else jumped in terror. They were having such a good time that they didn't notice that neither Beth nor Hunter spoke or reacted to any of the creatures.

Beth halted when the ghoul in a dirty karate gi stepped forward. He lifted the velvet rope and blocked their way to the left.

The ghoul stared at her. She remembered seeing him in the Cabinet of Souls, but did he remember her? Was he trying to give her a message? Or was it all in her imagination? She couldn't guess.

The ghoul didn't move or speak. She looked back at Hunter. He shrugged. It was her choice to go to the right, even if he pointed to the left.

She took Hunter's hand and steered him to the hall on the right. She couldn't stop now. The Cabinet of Souls—the real one—was hidden in there somewhere.

Beth and Hunter went through a door and into another corridor. Thick fog clung to the floor, moving only when they waded through it. They came around a corner and into a hall that looked unfinished. Plywood covered one wall, instead of the brocade wallpaper in the other hallways. There was a skeleton outside the door. He looked totally fake. Even his glowing eyes looked phony.

Nobody else was in sight.

"Maybe we took a wrong turn?" Beth said.

"I don't know." He pointed to another hallway on the left. "Let's try down there."

Beth nodded and led the way around the corner. This one was more brightly lit, but still dim enough that shadows crawled out from the walls in every direction. Then she he saw a marquee with Dr. Hysteria's face and the words MAGIC THEATER.

Hunter stepped past her and pushed the curtain in the doorway aside. He peeked in. Then motioned for her to step inside.

She walked through the door, hoping to find something that might lead them to her friends.

She was running out of time. It was getting late. It was probably past ten o'clock by now.

One thing Beth knew for sure: If she didn't find her friends before midnight, she would never see them again.

CHAPTER 28

BETH AND HUNTER WALKED DOWN
the center aisle of the small theater. She looked at the
stage and frowned. What sort of shows did they do here?

As if in answer, lightning flashed in front of them.
The theater filled with fog. When it cleared, Beth was
looking at herself standing on the side of a great chasm.
She was dressed like a princess in a fairy tale. A narrow
wooden bridge spanned the chasm. Her side of the chasm
was draped in gray shadows.

The other side of the chasm was filled with sunlight
and color—a perfect paradise. Then Hunter emerged
from the trees. He wore a brown leather outfit, like something Robin Hood would wear. His long, dark brown coat
dropped to the top of his boots. He was more handsome
than ever. A true prince, ready to win her heart.

Hunter held out his hand from his side of the bridge.
"Come over to this side, Beth. It's beautiful here!"

Beth was ready to leave her grim forest with its leaf-less trees. She wanted to meet her prince in the sunshine.

"Join me!" he urged, his dark eyes holding her gaze.

She held out her hand. "I will."

But before she could move, her friends burst out from among the trees. Nicole. Luke. Kellen! They were dressed in fairy-tale clothes, like her, but they sounded the way they had before they came to the Hall of Horrors. She could tell they were terrified.

"You can't go over there," Luke said, grasping her arm.

"You can't leave us," Nicole cried out.

Kellen took her other arm. "We need you."

"You're free without them," Hunter said from the other side of the bridge. "This is where you belong. It's who you really are."

No! The real Beth knew something was horribly wrong. She looked at Hunter. "No, that's not who I am."

She tried to look at her friends, but the vision wouldn't let her look away from her mirror self. The Beth in her vision raised her skirts and walked to the bridge.

"This isn't right," the real Beth told Hunter.

Fairy-tale Beth stepped onto the shadowy side of the bridge. She took one step, and then another. She was moving to Hunter's side . . . moving into the sunlight and color. Moving where the real Beth didn't want her to go.

The Beth in the vision stopped and looked back. Her

friends were reaching out to her in desperation. They were afraid for her as well as for themselves. The choice she made would affect them all.

Her gaze lingered longest on Kellen's face. Her friend, the one she always had been able to depend on . . . She realized how special he was to her.

Kellen had never steered her wrong.

Fairy-tale Beth looked out at the real Beth standing in the theater. The choice belonged to her.

"Your friends are holding you back," the real Hunter said. He moved closer to her.

Beth pulled away. "Your fairy tale is beautiful," she said. "But I would never betray my friends like that." She turned her back on the vision. It didn't seem beautiful anymore. It was as creepy as everything else in the Hall of Horrors. "I'm going to get out of here."

She walked out of the theater. Hunter grabbed her arm.

"Beth." He pointed at the curtain, a strange, angry look on his face. "We should go back in there."

"No! What's going on in there is obviously some kind of sorcery. It's wrong."

"It's showing us what we could be. The two of us. Together."

Beth stared at him for a long minute as the facts she'd ignored began to come together in her mind.

She asked him a simple question: "Who are you?"

CHAPTER 29

"DON'T BE STUPID, BETH," HUNTER

said, that odd expression still on his face. He was talking to her as if she were a child.

"Showing loyalty to my friends is *not* stupidity, Hunter," Beth replied coldly.

"How about your loyalty to me?" he snarled.

"I don't owe you any loyalty."

His eyes looked wild. Beth suddenly had the feeling that he wanted to grab her by the throat.

Before he could speak, Lilith stepped out of the shadows to stand by his side. "What's wrong, brother? Isn't she cooperating?"

"Brother?" Beth was shocked. She had never imagined anything like this.

Hunter ignored Beth and spoke only to Lilith. "No, she's not cooperating. She's being a stubborn little fool."

"Calm down, Hunter," Lilith ordered him. She turned

to Beth. "He didn't mean that. He cares about you, Beth. We all do."

Beth looked from brother to sister. Evil burned in their eyes. Evil, and something else.

Hunger.

"Get away from me!" Beth shouted. She turned and ran down the hall. She had to find her friends—now.

The corridor in front of her was empty. She ran until she reached a door. She flung it open and rushed into a witch's lair.

Inside, the witch was hunched over a cauldron. She was a hideous hag. Her ugly face was filled with warts, and her nose was curved like a bird of prey's beak. Her hair was stringy and tangled. But even so, Beth knew immediately that this monster was her friend Nicole.

The witch was hunched over a bubbling cauldron that gave off the most awful smell. Beth didn't want to think about what was inside.

Lightning flashed. It was so bright Beth felt it was going to blind her. Nicole cackled with delight. The audience members touring the Hall of Horrors were thrilled by her show. Beth was the only one who knew it was real.

Beth pushed into the center of the crowd as the witch cried, "Where's my broomstick? Who stole my broomstick?"

The younger kids beside Beth giggled nervously, but even they were having a great time. They cheered when a crooked stick fell into the hands of a ten-year-old boy. He looked at it in awe and fear.

"Wait a minute," called the witch. She stormed around the cauldron and pointed a bony finger at the boy. "You stole it!"

"No, I didn't!" said the frightened boy.

Beth watched in horror. Nicole never would have scared a little kid that way. Her transformation was more than physical. The girl she used to know had vanished into the evil soul of a witch.

The hag raised her hand and pointed again at the boy. "I curse you!"

There was a deafening bang of thunder and a cloud of smoke.

The boy was gone!

Nicole laughed and held out her hand. She opened her fingers slowly, and Beth could see that Nicole was holding a toad. She handed it to the boy's mother. "Here's your boy."

The parents gasped in shock.

"Nicole! You've got to get out of here!" Beth shouted.

The witch stared at her as if she'd never seen her before. Waving her hand, she shouted, "Clear the way!"

She picked up the broomstick, got on it sidesaddle, and rose up into the air, cackling with fiendish delight.

Beth watched as her friend vanished.

Suddenly, she heard Dr. Hysteria's voice, whispering, "Beth . . . Beth . . ."

She looked down at the stamp of Dr. Hysteria on her hand.

"You belong with us," the stamp hissed.

Beth looked away from her hand, toward the door. Lilith and Hunter were standing there, watching her.

Beth rushed to another door. She had to get away from them. She had to find her other friends. Maybe they would be able to help Nicole.

As she headed into the next room, she heard crazy laughter. Onstage was a frightening clown. Luke! The crowd cheered as he stormed over to another clown holding a balloon in the shape of a dog.

"I hate balloon animals," he snarled. He grabbed the balloon dog and held up a long pin.

Beth crept along the back of the room, never taking her eyes off her friend.

Pretending to be the balloon dog, Luke said, "No! No! Not the pin!"

"Shut up!" he replied in his own voice. "You're getting the pin!"

"No! No!" the balloon dog begged in its high-pitched voice.

"Too late!" Luke shouted.

He stuck the pin in the balloon dog. Green liquid gushed into a bucket by his feet.

The audience gasped, and Beth's stomach turned.

Laughing wildly, Luke picked up the bucket and threw the contents toward his audience. Except now, instead of goo, it was confetti.

As the audience applauded, Beth saw Hunter and Lilith stroll in. They were enjoying the chase.

She ran out into a corridor. Pausing to catch her breath when she reached another hall, she looked in both directions.

Two ghouls walked into the corridor to her right. They raised their arms and made a horrible, high scream as they moved toward her.

She turned and ran. She'd found Nicole and Luke. Now she had to find Kellen.

But where was he? She gasped as a terrible thought crossed her mind.

What if she was too late?

CHAPTER 30

BETH dUCKEd INTO THE NEXT dOOR-
way. Inside there was another show . . . if you could use
that word for such a cruel exhibition.

On the back wall, a huge banner announced THE
BEAST. In front of it, two goblins—one with a whip
and the other with a chair—were baiting a man-monster.
The beast roared out his defiance as Beth slipped into the
room.

The beast glanced her way.

Beth instantly recognized the creature's tortured eyes.
"Kellen!" She gasped.

The crowd and the goblins stared at her. She
ignored them.

The beast stopped. His face turned toward her again.
His gaze was longer this time. Beth felt that for a minute
she could see the real him. Could he see her?

She took a cautious step forward. "Kellen, it's Beth."

He growled, but not with the fury he had shown before.

"C'mon," she said. "You know me. Look at me. Look into my eyes."

She gazed at him, trying not to show any fear of the beast he had become. She shuddered to think about what would happen to Kellen if he didn't escape from the Hall of Horrors.

This time, he really looked into her eyes. She could see he felt something that wasn't rage.

"I know that's you," she said, hoping she was reaching beyond the beast, to Kellen.

He breathed heavily, but he held her gaze.

Maybe her name would trigger some memory in the part of him that was still Kellen. "It's Beth," she repeated.

Was she reaching him?

Suddenly, the door behind her opened. Hunter strode in and grabbed Beth's shoulders. "Okay," he crowed as he shoved her toward the ghouls. With a wide smile, as if it'd all been part of the act, Hunter said, "No trying to tame the monster, folks."

The audience chuckled, loving the "show." They began to applaud.

Beth ignored them. She ignored the ghouls holding her arms. She even ignored Hunter. All her attention was on Kellen, who stared at her, confused. Beth couldn't tell if he knew who she was. Had she reached him at all?

"Kellen! Please!" she cried over the applause. She begged again, more softly, "Please."

The beast's eyes changed, and he leaped at Hunter, grabbing him by the throat and throwing him to the floor. Cries of horror came from the audience. They scrambled to escape.

The beast left Hunter lying senseless at his feet. He had a new target. One of the ghouls rushed toward him, swinging.

The beast swung harder. He sent the ghoul spinning and crashing through the plywood circus poster. The ghoul landed on the floor, hard.

The other ghoul ran out of the theater along with the audience, terrified by what they'd seen.

The beast jumped down off the stage and ran to Beth. She didn't move. She wasn't afraid. She just looked at him, knowing that Kellen was someone she could always trust.

He put a claw gently on her back, and she let him steer her to the exit door. They left the place without a backward glance.

CHAPTER 31

BETH HELPED KELLEN DOWN THE hall. She could hear Dr. Hysteria's voice coming from the PA system: "Ladies and gentlemen, the Hall of Horrors will be closing in five minutes. Please proceed to the exits. We hope you have had a fun and thrilling experience."

Outside, the audience poured out the door into the night. Adults. Teens. Little kids. They all seemed to be enjoying themselves.

Mayor Smith walked out with his family. "Wow! That seems real! So real."

The mayor spotted Sheriff Wilson among the crowd and hurried over. "Oh, Sheriff, what did you think?"

"It was outstanding."

"I'm going to talk to them about coming back next year. It's been great for this town."

The sheriff nodded. "Well, it's almost midnight. I should probably be getting these kids home."

"Good night," said the mayor in his Dracula voice. "Count Dracula," he added, making sure everyone got the joke.

The two families headed down the street.

The minutes were slipping by as Beth tried to help Kellen along the corridor. It was nearly midnight. Time was running out.

Kellen reeled from one wall to the other, seizing pipes or anything else to keep him on his feet.

"C'mon," she urged, linking her arm with his.

Suddenly, he collapsed. His fight against the spell was taking a tremendous toll on him. He clutched his head and moaned.

"Kellen!" Beth grabbed his arm and helped him up as far as his knees. "Kellen, we have to find Nicole and Luke."

"Too weak." He spoke for the first time. His voice was raspy, but he spoke.

"Stand up for me," she said quietly.

He shook his head.

"I know you can do it," she said. "I know you have it in you. I need you to stand up for me. Right now!"

"Leave me," he struggled to say. "Save . . . yourself."

"No! I won't leave you. Please try." Tears filled her eyes. They had come this far. They couldn't give up now. Not when it was so close to midnight. "Kellen, please try for me." Her voice dropped to a whisper. "Please try. Please try for me. Kellen, c'mon. Please try for me."

He stared at her.

Tears ran down her cheeks. "I need you to do this for me."

He nodded.

She took his hand, hoping she could be of some help. He groaned as he fought his way to his feet.

They staggered together along the hall, but Kellen fell to the floor again. He got up, but now Beth was losing hope. It felt like they were going in circles.

Still, they kept on. They had to find Luke and Nicole before midnight.

Beside them, a door creaked open. Beth looked up. Dr. Hysteria, Lilith, and the creatures that were the trapped souls stood there. Beside them was the fiendish clown, Luke. And the witch, Nicole. Neither seemed to recognize her. Behind them was the Cabinet of Souls.

Beth slowly got to her feet, more terrified than she'd ever been.

"He was stronger than we thought," Dr. Hysteria said.

"That's good, Father," cooed Lilith. "That's good. Kellen's soul will give nourishment for a long time."

"Yes."

Beth gasped as a set of hands grabbed her from behind. Hunter had her in a chokehold. She fought him, but it was impossible. He was far too strong for her.

At her feet, Kellen could only watch. His last reserves of strength were gone.

"Hurry." Dr. Hysteria took out a pocket watch. "It's almost midnight."

As he turned away, Hunter half carried Beth into the room. The two ghouls grabbed Kellen and jerked him to his feet. They dragged him through the doorway and toward the Cabinet of Souls.

Dr. Hysteria glanced at Beth. "Bring her inside."

She struggled, but it was no use. Hunter pulled her closer and closer to the Cabinet of Souls.

She was doomed.

CHAPTER 32

THE DOORS OF THE CABINET OF

Souls swung open with a horrible hiss. Just as before, the creatures entered in two lines. The moaning grew louder as the monsters crossed over into the gray mist.

Hunter pulled Beth's arm and shoved her roughly inside. Lilith and Dr. Hysteria stepped in behind them.

Beth saw Nicole immediately. She was once again a pretty girl with great fashion sense. Now she stood frozen, gazing up at the ceiling like the rest of the trapped souls. The hideous witch approached her, then slowly merged with the beautiful young girl. Nicole's head dropped forward, and she stared straight ahead.

The clown disappeared into Luke, who shuddered but then dropped forward like all the others.

Beth gave a soft cry when the ghouls shoved the beast into Kellen.

"Oh, Kellen," she cried. It was horrible to see her

friends like this. Nothing she'd seen before had been this terrible. "Luke! Nicole! You guys, wake up!"

"They can't hear you," Hunter taunted her. "They exist now only to feed us."

The full horror of it washed over Beth as she realized that she would never see her friends again. That the three truly were demons.

Dr. Hysteria looked at Kellen. "That one was strong. He resisted more than the others."

"But you're the strongest, Beth," said Lilith.

"You're special," Hunter added.

"It would have been easy for you," Dr. Hysteria said, staring at her with his evil eyes, "to give in to temptation. To deny your friends for the sake of your own happiness. But you resisted. That's the strength we look for. Not in our food, but in our family."

"What?" Beth cried. "I don't want to be a part of your sick family!"

"Beth," cooed Lilith, "you'll live forever."

She shook her head.

"Nothing can save your friends," Hunter said.

"But you can save yourself," Lilith added.

Dr. Hysteria looked down at his pocket watch. It was 11:57. "It's almost time."

Hunter held out his hand, just as he had in her vision. "Join us."

CHAPTER 33

BETH STARED AT THE DEMONS, did they really think she'd give them a different answer this time? "No!"

She pulled a small water bottle from her sleeve, opened the top, and sprayed its contents at Dr. Hysteria, Lilith, and Hunter. They cried out in pain as steam rose from the places the water had struck them. It was as if the water burned them.

A powerful wind surged through the Cabinet of Souls, blowing outward from the demons. It almost knocked Beth off her feet.

All around her, the trapped souls shuddered. They began to move their arms. They turned their heads. They blinked.

"Guys!" Beth shouted to the young people in the cabinet. The wind was so strong that she struggled to stay on her feet. "Wake up! You're free now!"

The trapped souls glanced around, baffled and lost.

Dr. Hysteria laughed and held up his pocket watch. It

read 11:58. "It's too late! You and your friends are all doomed!"

Beth shouted to the trapped souls over the roar of the wind. "There's not much time. We have to get out of here!"

She turned and ran toward the door, beckoning the others to follow.

Kellen was the first to break free. He grabbed Nicole's hand, pulling her with him. Luke threw himself forward to catch Nicole's other hand.

Together again, the four friends tried desperately to reach the door. The wind pushed them back with each step.

As the demons continued to writhe in agony, Beth clutched the door.

"Beth!" shouted Kellen.

"Kellen!" She saw his hand and reached out her own, still clinging to the door.

He was too far away. If she released the door, she'd be swept back into the storm that was growing stronger with every passing second.

Another hand grasped Beth's hand. "Andrea!" she cried in astonishment. "Help me save my friends!"

Andrea stepped between her and Kellen and caught his hand, too. She was a bridge between the friends.

Fighting for every inch, they stepped forward.

Beth got out.

Andrea followed her . . .

Kellen pushed as hard as he could against the wind. It was enough to bring Nicole and Luke with him.

Kellen made it through the door. Nicole stumbled after him.

Luke fell through behind Kellen and Nicole. As he did, they all heard a clock chime somewhere deep within the Hall of Horrors.

It was midnight.

Beth, Kellen, Luke, Nicole, and Andrea looked back into the Cabinet of Souls. Huge red flames burst out from the doorway beyond, where the trapped souls had stood. The fire rose up and over the demons. It surrounded them and pulled them into it.

Lilith vanished first, then Hunter. Dr. Hysteria roared out in defiance, but soon he, too, was sucked into the flames.

The doors of the Cabinet of Souls slammed shut.

Beth released the breath she'd been holding. Around her, her friends and Andrea looked at one another in disbelief.

They were free.

"Okay," said Beth. "Is everyone okay?"

"Next time you try to convince me that someone is evil," Kellen said, "I'm just going to take your word for it."

She laughed with relief, but stopped when Dr. Hysteria's voice rang through the room. "You'll never get away with this."

She looked down at the stamp on her hand. "You're mine," the voice inside the stamp snarled. "You're all mine."

The voice sounded like it was drowning. It soon died away as she rubbed off the image with her thumb.

"What is that?" asked Luke.

"Some holy water, some sage, some vinegar, and a couple of other things," Beth said with a smile.

"How did you know how to do that?" asked Luke, impressed.

"I went online and looked up how to stop a demon," Beth said, shrugging.

Everyone laughed . . . until the building began to shake wildly. White light blinded them.

A moment later, they could see again. They were out on the street.

"Whoa!" Kellen said. "It's all gone."

Dr. Hysteria's Hall of Horrors had vanished. The town square was back the way it had looked before Dr. Hysteria set up his "show."

Beth heard someone giggling. She turned and saw Andrea. She was giggling as she touched her face. She couldn't quite believe that she had escaped.

"Who's she?" asked Luke.

"This is Andrea Payton," Beth explained.

"I'm free," Andrea said with a grin so wide her face could barely contain it.

"Why don't you give your parents a call?" Beth asked her, offering the girl her cell phone. "I think they're probably looking for you."

"Thank you." She hugged Beth.

"Y'know," said Luke, "I never thought my love of churros would lead me into this kind of trouble."

The four friends laughed, glad to be back together.

"You laughed!" Luke told Nicole.

"Okay," Nicole admitted. "Yeah, I laughed."

"The posse's back together!" Luke cheered.

"It's all because of you, Beth," Kellen said.

She smiled. "It was because of our friendship. It was stronger than evil." She laughed. "As corny as that sounds, it's true."

"I know," Nicole said. "Let's go back to my house. We'll find my little brother's Halloween candy and eat *all* of it. Okay?"

"That's what I'm talkin' 'bout," Luke said. He grabbed Nicole by the shoulders, turned her around, and started steering her down the street. "All right. C'mon. I'm starving."

"Cute," Beth said, looking at Nicole and Luke. They'd

make a good couple. She started to follow them, but Kellen called her back.

"I forgot one thing," he said.

"What's that?" she asked, stepping closer to him.

He answered her with a kiss.

When they drew apart, she looked at him and smiled. "Well, it's about time!"

They kissed again, longer this time . . .

EPILOGUE

BETH AND KELLEN ARE SO WRAPPED

up in each other, they don't notice the flyer for the Hall of Horrors blowing by in the wind. It surges up between bushes, swirling, twirling . . .

Finally, it floats to the ground. The wind dies down, but its roar does not.

A light flashes, but there is no one to see the flyer land. Where it touches down, there is something standing on the ground.

The Cabinet of Souls.

There is a burst of light . . . and the doors of the cabinet begin to vibrate and shake.

With a blinding flash of light, the doors of the Cabinet of Souls burst open. Whatever is hidden inside pours out.

Who will be the next to find it?

No one.

Yet.